STRANGE FRUIT

A novel by

TODD A. ATKINS

Taylor Publications
P.O Box 491322
Fort Lauderdale, Florida 33349

This novel is a work of fiction. Any references to real events, businesses, organizations, and locales are intended only to give the fiction a sense of reality and authenticity. Any resemblance to actual person, living or dead, is entirely coincidental

Cataloging-in-Publication Data is on File with the Library of Congress

Atkins, Todd A
Strange Fruit: a novel/ by Todd A. Atkins.
ISBN 0-9754139-0-2

Printed in the United States of America
May 2004
First Edition

November 1999

"Kenneth, I'm pregnant!"

August 1998

I had to get to Ocala. Daddy had been sick awhile, some say dying, but they don't know him like I do. He would never have complained about a "spell" as he called them, but Cousin Margaret thought it better to call me before things got worse. I vowed I wouldn't go back there, but since Mama died, Daddy really didn't have anybody else to see about him, anybody except me.

The Northbound train from Fort Lauderdale traveled along the Florida coastline. Equally spaced palm trees lined Interstate 95 where new exits empty into sophisticated gated communities and 18-hole golf courses. After three hours, the train stopped in Melbourne, a small retirement community south of Cape Canaveral where I'd transfer to a bus for the last leg of the journey to Ocala.

Upon arrival, a clean and courteous porter unloaded my luggage, lifting it high off the ground to avoid scuffing the finish. Before crossing the street to the bus depot, I slipped him a five-dollar bill in appreciation for his caution and care.

The bus was late, and while I waited for it I wondered if it would have been better to drive the Benz. I lease my car and I didn't want to be concerned with the backend cost of mileage or wear and tear. The savings, I thought, was worth the inconvenience of public transportation. That notion evaporated when I saw the flume, smelled the smoke, and heard the groan of the approaching heap. I prayed that it wasn't my ride.

The broken-down bus rattled up to the station. Even before it came to a stop, I saw that two of the tall, thin tires had been haphazardly patched on the sidewall, one patch reinforcing the other. When the bus came to a complete stop, I stepped closer to see just how bad the tires were. Up close, broken steel belts poked through bald, rubber skin. It was just another confirmation that this bus was no Trailway or Greyhound. I backed away to take in the entire ugly sight. Although it had been painted over, I could still read the faintly raised letters on its side: Birmingham's *Best City Line 1966.*

The door opened suddenly, belching out a nasty looking man in a way-too-small jumpsuit. He emptied both barrels of his nose and wiped what was left on his greasy sleeve before snatching my ticket. He was the bus driver, but the stench of gas hovering over said that he did more than steer. His duties also included cleaning and repairing the mechanical dinosaur. By the look of things he had neglected both tasks for some time.

"Ya headed to Ocala?" he asked. I read his nametag. *Gideon*. It was a good name for a good old boy whose accent was thicker than West Virginian beetle juice.

"Yes," I answered, cringing as he flung my Louis Vuitton luggage into the bus' baggage compartment. "Hey *Goober*, take it easy with the Louie. That bag costs more than this bus!"

Gideon climbed up the stairs and plopped down on his seat without saying a word. He gave me the deadeye stare before spitting snuff at my feet.

"*Mister*, in these parts bags is bags. We don't care what you paid for 'em. Now get in or get left. Don't really make me a difference." He revved the engine once as a warning.

I didn't like his tone, but I had to admit that I probably provoked him. I should have said sorry, but I didn't want him to think that it was okay to treat my belongings or me disrespectfully.

I climbed the stairs to the first platform, trying to dodge the puddles of shit-colored sputum while searching for a clean seat. Gideon put the engine into gear, popped the clutch, and then whipped the bus from the curb. The sharp turn flung me face first into the forth bench covered with cracked blue vinyl and rotting foam. On cue, it farted the foulest odor of unfiltered Pall Mall cigarettes into my nose and mouth. When I sat up straight, I saw Gideon's reflection in the rearview. He had my ticket in his free hand and a wicked glint in his eyes. "You all right?" he asked as he burst into irreverent laughter. "I'll be fine, *Gideon*," I humbly replied.

Gideon had gotten the best of me. It was practical justice, a fitting punishment for the offense. I had been rude and his response was appropriate. He was just trying to knock me down a few pegs, and rightly so. Thank God it was me and not my father he did this to because my father would have immediately called the thing an issue of race instead of what it was, a matter of respect.

During the journey back, I thought about how I'd matured since leaving Ocala in the 80s. I hoped and prayed that the citizens of Ocala had done the same. I dozed in 15-minute intervals on the way, waiting for signs, any signs, of growth and progress. Those signs never came. Instead, each hour on the bus was a fifteen-year journey back toward Mayberry, the black and white fictional town of Goober, Gomer, and Sheriff Andy Griffith. It's not that I expected Cappuccino and Stella Doro cookies, but a little sophistication would have been nice. When the three-hour drive was finally over, it seemed more like 1959 than 1999.

Chapter 1

The more things change the more they stay the same. Downtown Ocala was more alive than I remembered. Sun-dried white men dressed in overalls and banded straw hats leaned on the bumpers of vintage automobiles. To the Ocalans, '58 Chevys and '65 Fords were not the sexy status symbols treasured by Palm Beach socialites, but instead, reliable American transportation and work machines.

While I waited for my father, I remembered the number of times I'd pleaded with him to get a new truck, *new* meaning less than 15 years old. He answered me once around 1970, saying, "I'll get one when I need one." He had been driving the same beat up dually flatbed truck since I was four. I think it was Momma who told me that he bought it from Camden Murphy shortly after the accident that killed my brother.

I guess he *needed* a new one after Momma passed away, or maybe it was the insurance money burning a hole in his pocket. In any case, Pop bought a 1983 in late 1982. I saw it when I came home from college to bury my mother. It was top of the line, equipped with air conditioning, power windows and locks, and a big-block V8 engine.

When he finally drove up, I saw that the Chevy was still in great shape and shiny as ever. It was lower in the front than in the rear. All six of the tires were glazed and meaty. The vanity tag on the front end read: *Pissed Off Eight Days A Week.* Compared to the other vehicles dotting both sides of the street, my father's truck was flashy. It stuck out like a Baptist preacher at a Catholic rival. I hunched down as we made our way through town because for the first time I felt like we were uppity Negroes.

It took fifteen minutes before we made it to the house. Along the way, my father cut his eyes at me, sizing me up, it seemed. The truck had barely stopped rolling before he mumbled, "Go get my medicine from Reilly's Pharmacy." Before I knew it, he was out of the truck and inside of the house. His actions confirmed what I already knew: Pop had given an order to his son instead of requesting a favor of a man.

I took my time getting out of the truck, and time was exactly what I needed to remember that the man is my father and not one of my power mad med school professors. Once inside the house, his impatient huffs turned me around, and we made eye contact. Pop's face was fixed with the *hurry up you lazy bum* look he'd given me when I was a sensitive mama's boy in the late 60's, early 70's. He wore that expression a lot after Mathew died and I became an only child. Nobody, especially my father, understood how hard it was to live in the shadow of a dead saint.

"Mathew would have been back from the pharmacy by now," he muttered.

I was almost able to ignore his sarcasm, but he pushed and prodded me until, "I'm not Mathew!" bubbled unexpectedly out of my mouth.

I might as well have told him to kiss my ass because to a man like my father, backtalk was a challenge to his authority, fighting words as they say.

Pop postured and paced. He was the Alpha male and he was taking on challengers. I quickly lowered my gaze to the floor before he showed his teeth, but it was too late. He'd already begun to growl.

Pop puffed up like a viper. "You got somethin' to say? If you think you can handle the old man, c'mon with it!"

I softened my voice. "I have nothing to say, sir. Just leave the keys to the truck. I'll get your stuff in a minute."

He cocked his head to the side and locked his jaw. "You don't need the keys. It's a short run." He waited a minute just to check for late challenges from me; I had none either in my heart or my mouth.

After Pop backed out of the room, I found courage's reckless cousin named pride. My father could have killed me with his will alone, but it didn't matter. Kick any dog long enough and hard enough, it will bite. I'd had enough. When I found him in the living room my eyes darkened and I spat one icy word at a time from the angry part of my soul. "I'm a grown ass—" I started, but I caught myself before the venom came. Thank goodness he didn't hear that well.

That was not the way to settle differences between us. It is a short distance to the pharmacy, but I wasn't running anywhere for anybody, especially not Mr. Carnell Murphy. The sound of *his* truck rolling onto the main road let him know just what kind of man he'd raised.

Chapter 3

Reilly's Pharmacy was the only place in town still stocking Dr. John's Tonic. After searching the dusty shelves for ten minutes, I went to the counter for help. Mr. Clark was still working behind the window, bruised like an old pear, but still working. Anywhere else, Clark would be a museum exhibit with a plaque hanging from his neck that read: *Java man*. But in Ocala, he was as much a part of the pharmacy as the antique soda machine underneath the Norman Rockwell poster.

I knew Mr. Clark wouldn't remember me, so I didn't bother saying anything except, "Morning. Bottle of Dr. John's Tonic, please."

Mr. Clark paused as though thinking, then he slowly climbed the stepladder to reach the highest shelf. Once there he pulled a pasty, dust-covered bottle from it. His wiry arms and bony legs trembled while he came down the ladder. Back at the counter, the old curmudgeon looked like a weathered piece of driftwood.

The weight of the bottle was too much for Clark's frail arms. I could tell because he trembled as he handed the bottle to me across the yellowed linoleum counter.

"Need a bag?" he asked in his legendary surly tone.

"Yes, thank you." I turned the bottle round in search of an expiration date. "Is this still good?"

"Good? I wouldn't be selling it if it weren't good," he scowled. Old Man Clark hadn't changed a bit. He was still a short-tempered, brassy man who never smiled.

I held the dusty bottle up to the light in search of an expiration date. "No offense, but I don't see a date."

Clark sucked his teeth. "That's 'cause it don't need one. Still hardheaded Kenny, I see. Just give it to your daddy. He'll know what to do."

"How'd you know my name?" I was surprised that a man surely in his late seventies remembered me from the hundreds of black boys growing up in the area at the time.

Mr. Clark looked up at the nearly empty shelves where he stored the tonic. "S'only two men around still use Dr. John's: Camden Murphy and

Carnell Murphy. And you sure as hell ain't Camden's boy!"

"Amen for that!" I heard over my shoulder. I turned to see who it was. "And, I'll take a bottle of tonic, too. We may as well stock up."

"H'ya, Terri," said Mr. Clark, looking through me as though I was plate glass. "How's your daddy?"

"Still cranky," she joked. "Other than that, he's fine.

"A man after my own heart."

"You two antiques oughtta quit working." Terri leaned over the counter and whispered, "Ya know, you and Daddy have more time on the job than Colonel Sanders."

Clark's lips pulled back like leathery vertical blinds, revealing all four of his brown teeth. The three on the top were loosely planted in his shriveled gums, but the one on the bottom was strong and sure. In the 38 years since my birth, I had never seen Mr. Clark smile, let alone blush. Even at his age, he couldn't resist Terri's playful teasing.

I hadn't seen Terri in years, but couldn't help but remember her. She had that kind of face. Besides, she was her mother's daughter, a spitfire whose tongue cut better than a Ginzu knife. One way or another, she was unforgettable.

"Good Morning, Ms. Murphy," I said enthusiastically, not sure if she'd remember me at all.

"Mornin'," she flatly replied.

"I'm Kenneth Murphy. My father . . ."

Terri cut me off harshly. "—I know who your father is!"

"Excuse me," I said sarcastically. "I was under the impression that I was addressing a lady, but I see that I'm mistaken."

"No, I'm not a lady . . . But your daddy is," she wisecracked, while bulling past me.

"Hey, look, I was just trying to be nice, but you know what? You're not worth it."

"Then you should have stopped at good morning, you dumb bastard."

What's her freaking problem? I thought. She behaved like a girl with a grudge. It really didn't matter because my father taught us to give respect but never, ever, kiss ass. When I arrived back at the house, Pop wasn't surprised at all that Terri and I had gotten into it. His face said it all, so I really didn't need to hear his question: "Why'd you speak to that girl anyway?"

"Because it was the right thing to do, Pop."

"Well, Kenny, not much has changed around here since you left. It would be good if you remember that."

Just as I expected, his favorite *Murphyism* came next.

" . . . And stay with your own kind 'cause nobody likes gray, gray skies, gray hair or gray crayons. And that's exactly what you get when you mix white and black together." Thanks to a strong mother and a good education, I knew better than to buy into that.

I changed the subject before he went into his *history-according-to-Carnell Murphy* speech. I knew that most white people weren't members of the KKK or the Aryan Nation, but I really didn't want to take him on because I'd lose. In these parts, the tradition of ignorance was as common as oatmeal. And although I hated to admit it, Pop's views on race were well within the boundaries of Ocalan normalcy.

I pulled the bottle of Dr. John's Tonic from the wrinkled paper bag and placed it on the table.

"Pop, why don't you let me prescribe some *real* medicine?" My question interrupted his mumbled string of Colored complaints. It was clear that he wasn't particularly fond of Terri or the race to which she belongs.

I read the ingredients listed on the back of the tonic bottle. "I can't find anything on this label that will help you with any medical condition. What do you have anyway?"

Pop looked at his watch. "Son, what I got is old age. This tonic helps me. Just leave it at that."

"Yes sir."

"Now, c'mon let's go. I got to check on the workers. It's not the way it used to be. Lots of the pickers are Spanish; they don't understand a word of English, so I gotta point some things out."

Pop grabbed his wallet and keys. We locked up the house and entered the truck for the short drive to the grove.

The drive seemed longer than it had ever been. Pop coughed the entire trip to Murphy's Grove. It was twenty minutes on foot, eight minutes by truck. During the drive we heard a loud buzzing over the orange grove. White smoke trailed the low-flying, old plane.

"Crop dusting?" I asked.

"Crop dustin' and fertilizin'. I'm waitin' to see how long it'll take before they start pickin' oranges in them fly-bys."

My father didn't believe in change even if it brought about improvements. "Progress," he said in his jaded way, "is no substitute for keepin' your mouth shut and mindin' your own business."

"How's Mr. Murphy?" I asked just to make conversation. Pop didn't answer the first time, even though he'd turned his good ear toward me. He didn't answer until I asked again.

"I'm just fine," he said while checking the strength in his forearm.

"That's good, but I was talking about Camden Murphy."

Pop's face turned sour. "What'cha askin' 'bout him for?"

"Never mind," I said then quickly changed the subject. "Hey, what are you getting per basket of oranges these days?"

"As much as I can," he said, raising his eyebrows to let me know that his business was no business of mine. "I make a livin'."

He was proud and he had every right to be. He'd taken care of his family, sent me to college, and then to medical school. While she was alive, my mother never had to work a day outside of the home. And he'd done it all as an uncompromising business owner.

"You and Mr. Murphy still negotiate price in the spring?"

"Nope. His daughter's taken over the business. She used to come to see me. Now I just tell her my *take-it-or-leave-it* price by phone."

"Does she take it?"

"She has no choice."

"Why?"

"Her father makes her. Each year I raise the price and he 'cepts it like it's nothin'. Never was like that until . . .."

By the way Pop's voice trailed off, I knew that he was drifting to the past, recalling a former life and time. Whatever experience he found in his memory still stung. The pain was still tangible, as real as ever, somehow undiminished by time; yet, he found the strength to resist it. For dignity's sake he held it, held it in. His tongue tried to betray him even as he fortified himself, but he silenced it. He spoke no more until we got back to the house, a place that stopped being home for me after Momma died.

Chapter 4

Returning from Murphy's Grove, we drove into the yard and right up to the front door. We could have never done this if my mother were still alive.

Momma always insisted that Pop park the truck on the side or the back of the house. She said it was niggerish to park in front of the entryway even though the white folks did it all the time. When Pop told her that other people did it, she understood that *other* meant white people. "Never mind," she'd say to Pop. We are not like them. Lots of thing they do, we don't do, can't do, or won't do."

At the grove, we'd loaded a crate of oranges in the back of the truck. I exited the passenger compartment to fetch it, but Pop got there first. While I was still daydreaming, he'd gotten out of the truck's cab and walked to the back. He opened the tailgate and slid, butt first, onto the truck bed to reach the container that had settled close to the front during the drive. Pop pulled the crate to the edge and then lifted it into his arms. The oranges were heavier than he. While reaching for the crate of oranges in his arm, I said, "Let me take that." He pulled away to prove to me that thin doesn't necessarily mean weak.

Pop carried the oranges up the stairs to the outside door and used his foot to open the screen. I climbed the five steps up to the porch and tried again to take the crate from him, this time as a matter of practicality.

"If you want to help me, unlock the door," he said. I pulled back the screen door. "I would've never sent you to school if I wanted you workin' with oranges." Instead of showing his appreciation, he scolded me. I couldn't do anything to please him.

I put the key in the lock and turned, twisted the knob and pushed. The door flung open. Pop crossed the threshold into the house while I prevented the screen door from smashing into his back.

The floorboards creaked as we crossed the small parlor into the kitchen. Electrical wires were everywhere, raw and exposed. The kitchen light bulb dangled from a plant hook. The brown cords were like spider webs. I traced the cords with my eyes, but couldn't tell where they connected to the wall outlets, or even if there were outlets. Even though electricity was available throughout the house, Pop pulled the curtains to let in the fading sunlight. The east side of the house was already dark.

"Why don't you just switch on the lights?" I asked. It was a stupid question. There were no light switches in view because none were installed. The house had been built before homes were routinely wired for power. Pop lit kerosene lamps in each of the rooms. To redeem myself, I offered to take care of the problem.

"Tomorrow I'm going to call an electrician to properly wire this house."

"For what?" he asked through pursed lips. "We've lived here all these years just like it is."

He had a good point, but mine was better. "Because your son is a doctor and can afford it."

"So can I," he said, making it clear that he needed nothing from me.

I didn't expect him to refuse but he did just that, and it caught me unprepared. I noticed that he was still smarting from the offer, but I couldn't understand why. He took my good intention and, once again, somehow changed it to an insult.

"What? Can't I do something for my own father?"

"*If* I wanted this place wired, it would be wired already. Would've been cheaper than sendin' you to school."

It never dawned on me that he didn't want the convenience and safety of power, but that was my father's nature. Nothing he did was safe or convenient. He cut his own path. It wasn't until later, after my own experiences, that I discovered that stubborn single-mindedness was the wellspring of his strength—and weakness, perhaps mine, too.

I tapped him on the shoulder while he moved across the room. "You forgot to say, 'ignorant bastard.'" *Ignorant bastard* was the infamously hurtful tagline that he'd use whenever he talked to me. According to Pop, Mathew was the smart son; me, on the other hand, I was, well, just Kenny. The more he missed Mathew, the dumber I got.

Pop chuckled as if he and Momma were sharing a joke. Maybe he was. "I wasn't going to call you ignorant. I was gonna call you an *idiot*."

"Cut it out. It's not funny." Pop's words still pained me, and Momma wasn't around to protect me. As a child, I'd cry when he said such things to me. Momma made me feel better by telling me that 'Daddy is just trying to toughen you up.' It worked. It worked so well that we could barely talk to each other. It seemed kind of crazy to love him so much but like him so little. He treated acquaintances with more respect than he did me.

My father was respected, not liked, by all, mostly for his unwavering work ethic and even-handed logic. He'd managed to straddle the divide between whites and non-whites, but no one really knew exactly how. Colored people called him Mr. Murphy; white people called him Murphy; but nobody, I mean nobody, called him Carnell to his face, not even Momma.

He got along. He got along because he understood that he needed to work with what he had, in the there and then. But his greatest advantage was his understanding of people and their motives. Pop would tell people all the time, "A man will respect anythin' he can't control."

The noisy refrigerator, clunking and whizzing, took me into the past. I paused to look around the kitchen. Memories were everywhere. *No, things hadn't changed much*, I thought to myself. Across the small room underneath the window was the gas stove that was never without a cast iron pan full of fish grease sitting on top.

I hadn't noticed but Pop had switched on the burner under the frying pan; the tinkle of water evaporating from the oil confirmed it. He took the battered fish from the refrigerator and slid them slowly into the lard. I was in heaven. To black folk, there is something magical about the blended fragrance of fish, lard, and seasoned cornmeal. It makes us hum and dance in place.

I closed my eyes. "Mmm Home." When I reopened them, Pop was looking at me like I was on crack. I distracted him with a question. "Is the fish from the lake?"

"Nope, the river."

The smells, the sounds, the sights took over. They sent me back to memories and feelings I'd forgotten that I had, or better still, had put away long before.

I remembered how Pop sat in the kitchen watching Mama fry everything from fish to fowl. He looked so happy to just to sit and keep her company.

My brother and I always knew when dinner was ready by the changing scents wafting through the open windows and doors. Cornbread always went into the oven last. That was our final dinner bell. Mathew regularly got whacked for sticking his dirty fingers into the batter bowl or breaking off small pieces of crust from the finished masterpiece cooling on the window ledge.

Pop's voice brought me back from the past. Dinner was ready even if I wasn't. "It ain't as good as your Momma's cookin'," he said, as he took notice of the longing in my eyes. A shoulder pat comforted me, but still allowed him to maintain his image of strength. It was the best he could give under the circumstances. Over the years, I learned that when he wanted to, my father fit tenderness into the space between words.

We pushed our chairs to the table to eat. Before we began, Pop jumped up to get the lemonade and ice tray from the refrigerator. He cracked the ice in the tray with a pick, breaking the solid sheet into pieces to fill our large, mayonnaise glasses. When he returned to his seat, we bowed our heads.

In the city, I'd learned to thank God on the run. Prayer had long since lost its personal value for me. It had become merely a respectful acknowledgement of my parent's teaching. My recitation was quick and insincere. When I lifted my head, my father was staring directly into my eyes. I paid it no mind, and raised my fork to plunge into the crunchy fish. Except for a clenched jaw, Pop was statue-like, frozen like a three dimensional still life. He stared me down until I couldn't help but ask, "What's wrong?"

He dabbed his nose with the handkerchief he kept in his back pocket and then threw it on the table hard enough to overturn one of the drinking glasses. "You call that grace? This, *boy*, is your mother's house—not some uptown apartment overlookin' downtown Lauderdale. Have some goddamn respect!"

"I'm sorry," drizzled from my lips like red-eye gravy. I dropped my fork then forcefully swallowed what was already in my mouth. It stuck a little on account of the lump in my throat caused by my own brutish insensitivity.

Pop reached across the table to lock hands with me. There were three other place settings on the table: one in front of each of the two empty seats, and another sitting toward the center of the table that I thought was for fish bones. He looked at each of the settings before beginning his prayer.

"Lawd God, we come before you humbly givin' thanks for all that you have provided for us this day as everyday. We thank you Lawd for the blessin's you give, though we are unworthy to receive them. Father, we know that our loved ones eat at your table now; nonetheless, we remember them as you said to remember you. The settin's at the table are to remind us that family is always with us even when they've passed on. In the name of your holy son we pray. Amen."

One tired, burning tear rolled slowly over the skin valleys carved into my father's cheeks. It flattened in the gray stubble and then reformed at the jaw-line before landing on Pop's flannel shirt. He lifted himself from the table and mummied through the back door into the night.

I knew better than to follow. I, instead, took the time to preserve his food and drink. I reverently covered each dish with another and moved them to the stovetop to keep warm. The lemonade went into the freezer to slow the melting ice. He wouldn't be gone very long.

Daddy wept. To me, he had never been more dignified and courageous. When Mathew and Momma died, he didn't cry for them, not because he didn't want to, but because he couldn't. "A colored man," he said, "could never show his weakness and recover from it." To my father, crying was an unforgivable offense. Finally, he was strong enough to cry for himself. That used to be Momma's job.

Chapter 5

We made no mention of the night before. We had that type of understanding as Murphy men. An emotional display from any one of us was bad enough, but to talk about it put our code of silence in jeopardy.

Pop looked frail in the August dawn; the tonic hadn't worked. He dragged himself out of bed and into the kitchen for coffee, walking on the sides of his feet as though trying to avoid aggravating splinters stuck in his soles.

I gave him time to pour his first cup before approaching. He was hunched over the hot brew with his shoulders drawn toward his ear. "How'd you sleep?" I asked. That was our way of asking bigger questions without getting cussed out. He waved me off to avoid directly addressing the unresolved feelings hidden behind his iron mask.

"You're up late this morning." Late for Pop was five-thirty in the morning.

"Got no reason to be up early anymore. The pickers know to start before daylight. "'Sides, all I do is make sure they not pickin' the young oranges."

"Having a little trouble this morning?" I asked

"No more than every other sorry mornin'—Why?"

"It's just that you're moving like a three-legged turtle, that's all." Being in Ocala made me sound like them.

Pop tried to pick up his pace and balance his steps as he gathered his things for his morning shave and moved toward the bathroom.

The bathroom door had never been cut to fit the door. It was too small for the opening. Even with the door closed, there was a three-inch gap, which made privacy impossible.

I watched as Pop held his face down in the ceramic basin. He used his left hand to brace himself while his right hand stretched down his body to grab hold of the pain running up his side.

He lathered his face with soap and then took his straight razor and scratched the hairs from his cheeks, chin, and neck. Water pressure was low so rinsing was difficult. The open spigot spit water into his hand in bursts and pulses. I knew better than to ask Pop why he wouldn't fix the plumbing. I'd learned my lesson the night before so I just kept quiet and went to my room to dress.

I unpacked my belongings one at a time. Next I hung my pants in the small, dank closet and placed my shirts in the bureau drawer. Toiletries remained in my accessories bag, an expensive gift from an ex-girlfriend from Dover, Maine. In it was toner, clarifying scrub, and astringent, in addition to my shaving kit and anti-perspirant.

I squeezed some of the scrub into my hand and went to the kitchen sink to quickly wash my face before shaving. The scrub had a soft, powdery fragrance to it. I poured a cup of black coffee to mask the bouquet. After finishing the cup, I went to the bathroom to shave. I heard no sounds coming through the partially open door, so I assumed that Pop had finished and gone to his room. I walked in to find him stretched out on the floor, bleeding but conscious. His head was propped against the cast-iron tub.

"What happened?" I asked

"Don't know."

"That's a pretty good size bump you have there."

"Mm-hmm."

"Well, how long were you going to lay there?" I asked.

"Long as it takes," he replied

"Long as it takes for what?"

"For me to get up by myself," he concluded.

I examined him on the floor where he'd fallen. Other than the knot on his head, he looked fine. At 120 pounds, he was an easy lift. I reached down to pick him up, but instead he extended his hand. I took it and I pulled him toward his feet. Without his permission, a pain-filled "Damn!" escaped his lips. He later described the low, dull groan as a by-product of age.

Pop leaned to one side as though he'd been creamed with a kidney punch. He bent over, placing his hands on his knees like a winded athlete. I intentionally poked him in the side and waited for a response; there was little reaction. I slid behind him and tried again, this time pushing near the liver with a stiff, finger jab from my right hand.

"What the hell are you doin'?" he yelled. By his reaction, I knew he had some type of liver ailment.

"What's wrong with your blood filter?" That's what he called it when I was a boy.

"Nothin'. I told you that I'm old—tired, too. I'm entitled."

His words were labored. He fit half sentences between waves of pain. "What did the doctor say about it?"

"Hell, he's older than me. He understands age pains."

"Who's your doctor?" I asked

"Same doctor I've always had."

"Dr. Shaw?"

"The one and only," he replied.

"Dr. Shaw is no real doctor. He had a two-year apprenticeship after a stint in World War I as an army medic. Everybody knows that. No wonder you're in such bad shape."

Pop's eyes bulged then turned bloodshot. Through clenched teeth and tight jaw, he declared with Dirty Harry intensity, "He was good enough for your momma. Shaw saved a lot of lives when nobody else would."

"Yes, Pop, but times have changed." I picked up the phone and called Whitestone Memorial Hospital. "This is Dr. Murphy. I'd like to schedule my father for an evaluation. Yes," I said to the person at the hospital, "today."

Pop snatched the phone from my hand and slammed it to the cradle. The force sent the old rotary phone crashing to the floor. "Goddammit, I will not go to *that* hospital unless I'm already dead." He was trembling with anger. "Do you understand me, boy? Not unless I'm dead!"

What was I supposed to do? As a physician I knew that my father needed treatment; as a son, I could not overpower him. He wasn't my patient; he was my father. He was bleeding from a fall, the full extent of which I couldn't know without tests. He'd been seeing an old country doctor who had questionable skills and a mind dulled by the aging process. After checking my options, I did what any son would do. "Okay, Pop, okay, but what do we do now?"

"Hand me that bottle of tonic." Pop twisted the cap and filled his mouth. He wiped the excess on his sleeve and then slumped back into the settee. "I'll be all right. It just takes a few minutes to kick in." He sat awhile to regain his strength and his will.

"Go ahead and rest. I'll check on the pickers today. You just stay there on the sofa," I said, trying to be helpful.

Pop was seething. "How many ways I got to say it: I don't want you in the orange business!" He turned to look for his keys. When he found them he said, "I'm goin' to work." He rose to his feet in sections, unfolding each body part like a rusty mechanical device. When he was completely upright, he pushed the tails of his shirt into his blue jeans and then tightened his belt to accommodate his shrinking waistline.

"Why don't you listen to me? I am a real doctor, you know."

"You better be! Remember, I'm the one who paid the damn fees."

Pop took one step away from the sofa then crumbled to the floor in pain. I'd had it. I called the ambulance for the ride to Whitestone Hospital, the nearest legitimate hospital to the grove. Colored Hospital, renamed Charles Drew Medical Center, was closer, but black people ran it. Sadly, their incompetence was legendary. When I was a kid, it was a broken down, low-tech clinic that could barely keep tongue depressors on the shelves. Colored Hospital could have been twenty feet away, but I wasn't going to take my father there. He deserved better.

"Don't you take me to Whitestone Hospital. I'm not goin' to Whitestone. Not that p-place . . . " He faded quickly. "Please, son, don't . . . not White—" was the last thing he said before passing out briefly.

I lied to the EMS dispatcher, telling them that Pop's situation was no emergency. It was the only way that he could lawfully be transported twenty miles to the more distant Whitestone.

Whitestone Memorial Hospital was immaculate. I had never seen a hospital with brilliant-white plantation columns. The outside was a restored southern manor bedecked with lush green grass, cypress, and Florida oak. Inside, it was a modern medical facility. I read the plaque in the entryway. *Historic Site 1906. Renovated by the trust of Thomas James Whitestone beloved son of Ocala.*

Pop was triaged then admitted before being sent for x-rays, which gave me time to grab a snack.

I browsed the hallways looking for the cafeteria. The sea of pink and white faces made me think of a carnation garden. When I found the cafeteria, I ordered coffee. "Sugar and cream, sir?" asked the attendant behind the counter. I nodded yes and then sat to enjoy my coffee. To my surprise, they had Starbuck's blend.

A tray toppled over as an intern rushed to another part of the hospital. Within minutes, a pimple-faced eighteen-year-old wearing a Black Sabbath T-shirt was there with a bucket and a yellow caution placard.

After the commotion, I turned my attention back to food. I followed the spice trail to the kitchen area where I caught the scent of collard greens and ham hocks. I assumed that black folks were doing the cooking until I saw the white faces beyond the swinging doors. *White folks making collard greens*, I thought, *Pop won't believe this*.

Pop waited for me in radiology. His x-ray images had been shot shortly after he arrived there and he had already received his room assignment when I found him.

"I'm back," I announced. The female transporter bagging Pop's personal affects looked up at me then looked down to finish packing. The short, chubby woman looked more like a lunch server than transporter. "Y'all from here?" she asked while stepping to the head of the stretcher.

"Uh-huh," I replied.

Pop was looking up at the blinding, fluorescent lights and away from the stubby lady. He was detached but alert.

"Why do you ask?"

"Well, we don't get many black people at this hospital. When we do, most are from outta town," she said. She directed her next question to Pop. "Are you feelin' any better, Mr. Murphy?"

Pop's gaze ripped into the unsuspecting woman. His lips remained sealed. His hands were folded across his chest. He wasn't going to open up to her despite her effort to engage him. "He looks better," I said, jumping in so that she wouldn't think him rude.

"He don't talk much, huh? Did he fall and hit his head or sumthin?"

"Yes," I answered. Pop glared at me. His eyes scolded me for talking to yet another white woman. We were quiet until we arrived at Room 243A.

"Mr. Murphy," she said in a loud voice, while bumping the stretcher against the bed, "Do you think you can slide across on your own?"

Pop didn't answer, but I could read his thoughts. He was silently calling her ignorant. Instead of talking, he just slid across to the bed, adjusted the pillow under his neck, and refolded his arms across his chest.

"Hope ya feel better soon, sir. I'm sure Mr. Williams could use the company." Pop and I both looked at Williams. He was a bespectacled, stately man who looked like a Wall Street retiree. He gazed up from his *Business Week* to greet us.

"Gentlemen," Williams said.

"Morning," I replied. Pop said nothing, but acknowledged Mr. Williams with a quick wink of his eye and a tilt of his head.

"Not from around here?" I asked.

"No. I'm from Delaware. Decided I had enough of the city. Just bought 150 acres of farm and citrus. Fresh air, simple life."

"That's great. Nothing like it," I said

Williams looked down at my soft leather shoes and linen trouser. "You don't look like a local either."

"I am, but I've been away for some time. I've gotten use to weekdays in the city and weekends on the beach. I came back to Ocala to take care of my sick father.

"I see. It seems like as good a place as any for a sick person. The facility is beautifully equipped. I did the tour before being admitted. It certainly is much more than I expected for a rural town like this."

Pop's mouth creaked open for the first time since we arrived. "That's because this hospital isn't for us."

"Us? Us like who?" asked Mr. Williams.

"Colored people," Pop replied.

"Nonsense."

Pop gave Mr. Williams a sharp look of disapproval. "If you are as smart as you seem, you'd do better to get out of here as soon as you can."

Williams adjusted his glasses. "This hospital must serve everybody."

"And if they don't . . .?" Pop asked

"Why, litigation of course."

"Suin' takes lots of time and money. What do you do in the mean time?"

"I don't anticipate any problems. I have Blue Cross/Blue Shield Indemnity. It's the best insurance on the market."

"It doesn't matter. You're still colored and this is no place for you."

"My God, man, don't you know that money changes thing. The only color these people care about is green."

"Think so?"

"Sure."

"Then how come the two of us coloreds are stuck together in this room when there are plenty of empty rooms in this dump?"

The conversation was over as quickly as it began. Pop had heard all he wanted to hear from Mr. Williams, but he had to take a last shot.

"Take it from me Williams, all money does for you in this hospital is makes you a sick Negro with money."

Mr. Williams rang the bell and waited for the nurse to arrive. "I'd like a private room, nurse."

The nurse stood at the end of his bed and read his chart. She put on her gloves and took a pulse, pressure, and temperature. After discarding the gloves, she scribbled notes into the chart. Finally, she answered as she was leaving the room. "I'll see if we can find an empty room."

"I demand a private room! If my insurance doesn't cover it, I'll right a personal check." Mr. Williams was breathing fire.

The nurse kept walking, unaffected by Mr. Williams' demand or his ability to pay.

"See what I told you, son," said Pop self-righteously. "Now get me the hell out of here."

"Let's just wait until we get your results. Then we can leave," I said.

"Don't need them."

I sat down. "Why not?"

"I know what I got."

"Yeah?"

"What's that, Pop?"

"Bad liver."

"How do you know that?"

"I know. Now, can you help with my pants? I'll feel better once I get home, or at least away from here."

I kept probing. "Okay, but what do you mean by bad liver?"

"My liver isn't workin' like it's supposed to. What part of that don't you understand, Mr. Doctor."

"Did Doc Shaw tell you this or did you diagnose yourself?"

"I don't need somebody else to tell me what I already know," he said adamantly.

"Pop, we're not leaving until we get your results back. I'll call the doctor."

Pop put on his pants by himself and perched on the edge of the bed. Twenty minutes later the resident came to give us the news.

"Mr. Murphy, you have severe liver shrinkage. It's malfunctioning pretty badly."

Pop heard enough. "See, I told you. Let's go."

"Just give the man a minute to finish, Pop. Is there more, doctor?"

"Yes. It appears to be cirrhosis. We also found unusually high levels of phosphorous, nitrogen, and ammonia in his system, which may have contributed to his condition. We're going to need to run more tests."

Pop cut in. "No more tests. Nurse, please call me a ride. I just want to go home."

"Anything else?" I asked the young doctor.

"We found opiate by-products in his blood and urine samples."

I turned to my father for an explanation. "What is this man talking about?"

"He's about as dumb as you," he said, then he walked away, bracing himself by holding on to furniture as he moved toward the exit. He rested on the wall for a few seconds. "You comin'?"

"You'd be leaving against medical advice, Mr. Murphy."

"Yeah, yeah, yeah. I got a doctor at home."

"You're going to need to sign some release papers."

"The hell I will. My signature ain't gonna be on none of your papers."

"Doctor, you can release him to my care and custody. I am a physician."

The resident looked up from his clipboard notes with concern. "He needs care. You shouldn't let him leave until we've finished our assessment. Based on the initial report, he's in pretty bad shape. He could die."

I turned to speak to Pop, who had already shuffled to the door. "Do you hear that? You could die."

"I heard. I'm old enough to die. That'll be fine with me."

"I know I don't have to tell you that you shouldn't be treating your own father. Why don't you leave him in our care? I can assure you he will receive the best this hospital has to offer," said the resident while making a notation in the progress note.

"I understand, but do you want to try to stop him?" I asked.

"We could Baker Act him."

"How is that? He's competent."

"Your father has enough morphine in his system to drop a large rhino. We could make a case that he is attempting to kill himself."

"He'd never forgive me, or for that matter, get over the stigma. I'm sorry. I'm going to take him home."

"I don't advise it, but it's your call."

"No, it's his call."

Pop scooted up the hallway toward the exit. He never looked back. I came up behind him and supported his weak side to the portico. We could have taken a taxi back to the house, but he insisted on taking the bus. We waited nearly forty-five minutes before one came.

Chapter 6

Pop slept the rest of the day. While he was sleeping I went to the grove to spot-check the pickers and do some quality control.

At the grove, baskets were everywhere. The pickers were working diligently. I grabbed a few samples from each of the baskets to verify ripeness. As far as I could tell there wasn't one young orange in any of the containers. I continued to walk the property and ended up near the processing plant and office. Two figures were looking out the window at me, but I didn't pay them any mind.

Pop's truck was at the far end of the grove. When I was satisfied with my survey, I turned to walk to the truck, taking easy strides. Ten yards into the short walk, the office door burst open and I heard a familiar voice.

"You, hey you!" Terri yelled as she stomped toward me through the loose dirt, kicking up a pretty good cloud of dust as she approached.

"What do you need? Make it quick Terri; I'm busy." Terri didn't like being rushed. I could tell by the look on her face.

"What kind of goddamn business do you think we're running here?" She shoved a small, dry orange at me. "You call this quality control? I could do a better job in my sleep."

I quickly examined the orange and then tossed it back to her. "Sorry, one must have gotten away."

"One got away? That's all you have to say? We pay *you people* good money to make sure that this doesn't happen. If I wanted juvenile oranges, I'd have picked them two months ago. I don't know why we keep you around. You Murphy's are worthless."

I warmed into a cheeky smile. "Last I recall you're a Murphy, too. Never know, we could be related. You know, rumor around these parts is that your granddaddy had a little thing for dark meat."

"You nasty little booger. We used to own your people. No true Murphy would be mixed up with the help."

I could tell she wanted our exchange to continue. I was just unsure about her motivation.

"Find someone else to play with. If you're finished, there's work to be done." I turned to walk away.

"I'm not finished with you," she said. It was prophetic. "Where is Carnell?"

"Carnell? Since when are you and my father friends? Mind your manners little girl. And from now on, you talk to me—understand?"

"—You're fired! Get your ass off our land. I can handle the pickers myself," Terri said

"Hey, wait a minute; you need me."

"Who says?"

"I do." I turned and yelled to the workers in the grove, speaking to them in Spanish. *Finish the last basket and then go home. I will pay you in the morning. Tomorrow we're going to work on the Smith Grove. Come to my house in the morning.*"

"Thank you, Mr. Carnell's son. *Gracias*," said one of the workers who then gestured for everyone to follow him off the property.

"See you *do* need me. I just proved it."

"Get off our land, now!" Terri pulled a twenty-two-caliber pistol from her pocket.

I wasn't scared. "What are you going to do with that snake killer? You'd run out of bullets before I was dead. I've seen better BB guns."

"Put it away, Terri. Now apologize to the man." Camden Murphy spoke from the office doorway. His neatly cropped hair was white as snow. He had deep experience lines in his face—just like my father. "You ain't got to like him; you just got to work with him." He was limping badly as he pivoted slowly and returned to the innards of the office.

"Sorry," she mumbled like a rotten child. "Just have your men here in the morning." Terri walked toward the office door, undoubtedly to protest to her father.

She looked much better walking away. "Oh, and Terri? You've got to have a little sistah in you. I've never seen a white woman with a finer back porch swing."

Terri flipped the bird and then mouthed a nearly silent "Screw you."

"I'd love to. How about tonight? I'll put Pop to bed early and we'll have the whole house to ourselves," I said playfully. If this had been a few years earlier, I would be hanging from a Florida oak. I headed back to check on Pop.

When I arrived back at the house, he was sitting on the back porch. The sound of his truck probably woke him long before I pulled up. I parked on the side of the house like Momma had said to, then walked around to the backyard to think.

"Where you been?" he asked

"Murphy's Grove."

"What for?" Pop asked, filled with innuendo.

"I was just trying to help."

"Help do what?"

"Just went to check on the workers," I said but he didn't believe me.

"Anyone in particular?"

"No, why?" I asked

"I think the city's given you a taste for white meat—ain't that right?"

"No. I just went to make sure the pickers were doing the job the way it's supposed to be done. I'm trying to help keep things running around here until you get back on your feet."

"So you sayin' you've never had a white woman?"

I didn't know what to say. I knew the answer he wanted, but I still didn't know what to say without backing into one of his word traps.

"Pop, I'm an adult. You raised me to be a man. I make my own choices."

"I told you and your brother to stay away from them white folks. Y'all didn't listen then, suppose you won't listen now."

"It's not like I'm going to marry one," I said, as though my confession would ease his mind.

"I bet that's what O.J said, too. See what messin' with white folks got him."

"That's different. He forgot himself and where he came from. "I'm in control of my shi'—I mean stuff. No woman, white or otherwise, is ever going to get me again." A long pause and a heavy sigh came from the deepest part of my father. No matter how I talked, he knew there was no weight to my vow.

"When are you goin' back home, boy"?

"Are you trying to get rid of me or something? All I did was come to check on my sick father and this is the thanks I get."

"You think you're smart, don't you boy? You ain't that smart. Don't you know that the big snakes live in the country? They'll swallow your dumb ass up out here."

"I'm too smart for that," I said.

"You think those books or your fancy title will help you out here? You're dumber than I thought. Take that Terri girl . . ."

"What about her?

"She thought college was gonna let her take over Camden's business. She was wrong. Who do you think is callin' the shots right now?"

"I know what you're going to say."

"Her Daddy is still in charge, that's who. She can't buy a bag of bullshit without his consent, and he got 'bout as much education as me, which ain't sayin' much."

I countered, "That's because she works in her father's business. She'd have a lot more respect if she went to work somewhere else."

"That's partly right. The other reason is that this is still Ocala; not much has changed here in forty years. Forty years from now it'll be 'bout the same. That's why I got you out of here."

"I left for college. You didn't get me out of anywhere."

"Believe what you want. All I know is that you don't live here and that's just the way we planned it."

"Who are we?" I asked.

"Your Momma and me," he answered

"Can I ask you a question?

"Ask all you want. Don't make me no never mind."

"Did you always want me to be a doctor?"

"First tell me how much money you make a year?"

I tried to be cool. "About 140K. Why?"

"Because, I make the same money you do, and I didn't spend a day in college," he said proudly.

"If you thought school was such a waste of time and money, why'd you send me to college and medical school?"

"Your Momma sent you. She thought that if you turned into a doctor, you'd be above all of this color crap. She took Mathew's death real hard. She didn't want the same thing that happened to him to happen to you. I paid the school fees, but I knew you could never get away from being black, no matter how much education you got. Black wasn't the problem in the first place."

"Well, what was?"

"Fear was, son."

I thought about Mathew while Pop talked about me. "Mathew wanted to be like you. He used to tell me he was going to take over your business and then everybody would call him Murphy or Mr. Murphy."

"Softly Pop said, "I know. Mat thought he owned the grove, acted like it, too. When I told him that we didn't, he came up with a plan for us to buy it. He was only six then. That boy had so much sense he was scary."

"What's that suppose to mean?" I asked.

"Murphy had an engineer workin' on his orange press. That damn boy asked the man how much he could make as engineer workin' on presses. The sonuvabitch told him that nobody'd ever hire a nigger for that kind of job. From that day on, he planned to take over my business. Mathew wouldn't stay out of the proccessin' plant 'cause he wanted to know how everything worked." Pop started to get misty again. "Those no-good crackers killed my boy. Can't even trust the one's you think are okay."

"You can't say that, Pop. You ought to know better than to lump them all together. How do you like it when they call all niggers lazy?"

"That's fine with me when it's true. Niggers *are* lazy, but we're not niggers; we're colored. Colored people work hard. I didn't say white folks killed your brother; I said *crackers* killed him, and then sent your mother to an early grave over heartbreak. If you want me to forgive them for that, *so help me God,* it'll never happen."

Pop mustered his strength and headed for the woods. He looked healthy and strong walking into the setting sun through the brush surrounding the house. Anger had a way of charging his battery.

I went inside. Momma's photograph sat on the old piano. I banged a few chords out of *Amazing Grace* while trying to remember Momma's favorite spiritual. She'd sit at the piano and tell the story of how her parents endured Jim Crow laws at the turn of the century. The song, her song, was *A Closer Walk With Thee.*

Momma was looking back at me from the photograph of her and Mathew on top of the piano. I lifted it from its place so that I could be closer to her—so that she could hear the questions that I had to ask. "What do I do now, Momma?" The corners of her lips turned upward in a subtle smile and I knew that Momma was pleased that I'd come home to look after her husband, my father.

Chapter 7

I made orange marmalade chicken for dinner. Pop was still too sick to cook, so he came to the table without complaint. He really didn't want dinner, just the spoon so that he could take his tonic.

He was a practical man and it showed in everything he did. Right after blessing the table, he picked some of the orange slices from the chicken and ate them first. I don't think he really knew what to do with the rest of the meal. It was much different than the food he normally ate.

The napkins were folded into little linen blossoms growing from the bone china. While at the market, I'd bought fresh-cut flowers to put on the table, just to brighten the drab kitchen. I used the good silverware and glasses. Instead of putting all the food in the same plate, we ate in courses like civilized people. I thought that Momma would be pleased to know that.

The first course was the marmalade chicken. I plated two good-sized breasts with biased cut carrots. The ginger, cumin, and cloves made for a robust blend of fragrances and flavors. The snap peas were fanned across the marmalade base in a beautiful presentation. The second course was wild rice, which sat in the crock-pot in the center of the table where the empty plate had been the night before. Pop said nothing.

I unfolded my napkin and placed it on my lap. Then, I began to cut thin slices of the delicate chicken breast before taking up green beans and chicken with the fork. Pop didn't move. After a few bites and a swallow of fruity white wine, I gazed up from my plate. He still wasn't moving.

"How do you eat this stuff?

"Any way you want. It's just food," I answered.

Pop drew the rice cooker toward him and began to ladle two or three spoons of rice into his dish. He shoved the snap peas to the side after tasting them. The color of the peas and their sweet aftertaste were intensified by the cold-water bath that I'd given them. To Pop, the greens were just cold and undercooked. He brushed off the sauce and stabbed the whole chicken breast with his fork, tearing large chunks off with his teeth instead of cutting it into pieces with his knife.

Paper towels were on the table. He reached for one to wipe the sticky sauce from his lips. "Rich," he said, and then continued to tear at the chicken. He tried the wild rice. It was good Pop said, "except for those little hard things in it." He didn't touch his wine. Instead, he filled the mayonnaise jar with lemonade. He was curiously satisfied by the meal. "Where'd you learn how to cook like that?"

"Friends," is all I'd say.

"They can't be colored because colored folk don't cook like that. Your Momma would have really enjoyed this. She had a sweet tooth, and enjoyed a little frill every once in awhile."

"I'm glad, Pop."

"Too rich for my blood, though. You could've fried some chicken and boiled a few ears of corn. Now, that's food," he paused, "good enough to make me slap that English cookin' lady."

"She's not English. She's from up North."

"Sounds like one of them Brits to me, with her funny accent."

That's how it was between us. I'd say one thing, and he'd say another. I'd say something else, and he'd have to have the last word. Over the years, I'd learned to say, "You're right, Pop," just to have peace.

"You shouldn't be wastin' this uptown food on me. This is what you do for a woman you interested in. Why don't you go on home and find yourself a girl? I can take care of myself," he said, as though I needed a reason to leave.

"Pop, I know you can take care of yourself; that was never in question. You're in an awful hurry to make me leave, aren't you?"

"I wouldn't say that, but I know you have to get back to work. Life goes on."

"By the way, what kind of doctor are you?"

"A very good one."

"Who says?"

"Everybody."

"Everybody who?"

"My patients. I'm a surgeon."

"I thought surgeons make big money."

"They do when they get a lot of work. My hospital doesn't do much surgery."

"Then why don't you move to another hospital?"

"I could *if* I wanted to. I like my practice just the way it is. It's a small practice, but it takes care of my needs."

There was a long pause while Pop thought deeply. He would always cross his arms over his chest when he was deep in thought.

"Why surgery?"

"Don't know. It might have been something Momma said when I was finishing high school."

"What did she say?"

"I can't remember exactly but it was some thing about the power to change lives—I remember now. She held my hands close to her heart and prayed that God would use my hands to save and change lives. It's been a long time since I thought about that day. We were on our way to church. It was a memorial service for Mathew, if I remember correctly."

"I don't remember that," Pop said.

"You wouldn't. You had stopped going to the annual memorial service. I think that's when you started going into the woods. Momma said you just needed time to think and grieve alone. She said you had a special place that you'd go to remember Mathew—Do you still go there?"

"Yup, but not as often."

"Where do you go?"

"The lake. Mathew loved it there."

"Can we go together before I leave?"

"It's not a good idea. The lake is not like it used to be. It's dirty; it doesn't sparkle like it used to. It's a sad place now, a place of misery and mournin'. I don't even fish there much anymore.

"Is that right?"

"When I die you ought to sell this place and never come back here again."

"Why?" I asked. It didn't seem right to sell heir property.

"'Cause I said so. Besides, it's what your Momma wanted. Like you said, you're a man now and you can do what you want. But I'm still your father, and I'm telling you that Lauderdale is a better place for you than this ol' raggedy town."

"I hear you. What about our trip to the lake?" I asked.

"Well, when are you leavin'? We'll go there just before you leave—maybe."

"Just one thing, I am not leaving you alone until you're better or dead. Either you come back to Fort Lauderdale with me, or I stay here with you."

"I'm not going anywhere, Kenny. This is my home. You go on without me. You've spent the better part of your life away from here. Don't stay on account of me. This place has a way of sucking you back in."

"Back into what?"

"Into livin' and dyin' here. We've—our family, I mean, has been here a long time. Lots of mem'ries here. I know it's hard to let go."

"Not me. I can leave and never look back, Pop. Believe me, this is temporary. I'd be on the first thing smoking back to Lauderdale if I didn't have to worry about you."

"Don't worry about me son. I told you that this is my home; I'm not leavin'. I plan to die right here. Plant me in the backyard with your Momma and Mathew. That's the way it ought to be. I don't have much time. I'm not gonna waste it on movin' to the city at my age."

"Then you leave me no choice. I'm staying as long as it's necessary. Better or dead, remember?"

"Son, nobody will fault you for gettin' back to your own life. I'll be fine. Don't you got some lady to get back to?"

"I'm seeing somebody, but not seriously. She can do whatever she wants. I just got rid of the wife, and it cost me a pretty penny. I don't need a woman right now for anything but, well, you know."

"Don't get down on marriage. It's a holy institution. Your mother and I would still be happily married if she hadn't passed on."

"I know. I wasn't that lucky. My wife wanted a doctor, not a husband. The divorce almost cost me the practice. I have to pay her five years of alimony based on my salary. That's one of the reasons I don't want more business. She's having a good time on my sweat. They don't make good women like my Momma anymore. I think you got the last good one."

"She got any white in her?" he asked.

"About as much as either one of us—why?" Where are you going with this, Pop?"

"She looked awfully light to me," he said.

"Her grandfather on her mother side was white, I think."

"That's the problem. Start mixin' bloods and what you get is confusion. That's why I wanted a brown woman with chocolate fillin'. You couldn't pay me to fool with anythin' else."

"Pop, just about all of us have some white in us. The only place to find a real black woman is Africa."

"And what's wrong with that?"

"What am I going to do with a bush bunny, Pop?"

"What you mean is what's a bush bunny going to do with you? Listen, boy, colored women didn't get so good at wifin' and motherin' by accident. It's in their blood, passed down like that nappy hair on your thick head."

"You figured all this out on your own?" I asked, facetiously.

"Laugh if you want to, but it's true. You don't have to teach a rooster to crow, a fish to swim, or a horse to run—do you?"

"I suppose not, but we're not talking about chickens, fish, and horses. We're talking about people."

"People *are* animals, dummy and animals take care of their own kind, nothing or nobody else matters. You saw it yourself. That nurse had no right treatin' Williams like that, but all she saw was two colored men dirtyin' those pure white sheets."

I couldn't deny what I saw, but I could explain it. "She's ignorant like most of the people around here. You act like them; you become them. I'm telling you, sooner than later, progress is going to catch up with this town."

"Keep hope alive, son. What you callin' progress, son? Are you talkin' about white folks and black folks livin' together and gettin' together, but still bein' apart? That's not progress. That's curiosity, like turnin' over a rock that you know got bugs under it."

"I can't agree with that, Pop."

"You don't have to. My job is to tell you what I know. You can do what you want after that. I can't raise you twice. If you only knew . . ."

"Knew what, Pop?"

"Never mind. You'll learn. Your Momma used to say, 'a hard head makes a soft bottom.'"

Chapter 8

Pop was better the next day. He said Dr. John's tonic was responsible for his recovery. I didn't believe it. He just wanted me to go home before I got in some trouble; I could tell.

I convinced him to stay in the truck while we drove through the grove. He waved and several of the workers came up to him. "Feeling better? Good," they'd say to him. Pop had picked up quite a bit of Spanish from working with the migrant workers for many years. He said a few words in Spanish whenever he could get them in. They'd speak so fast.

Camden Murphy was standing in a clearing. I parked the truck so that the passenger's side was closest to him before jumping out to talk.

"Looks like a bumper crop this year."

Camden braced himself on his walking stick with two hands and leaned forward, fixed on Pop's position in the truck, looking but saying nothing.

I tried to engage Camden. "We should have those trees stripped of all the ripe oranges in ten days or so." He adjusted his glasses. They had fallen to the tip of his nose as he dropped his head to see into the passenger compartment, twisting his head so that the direct sunlight didn't blind him.

I tried again. "We've got great pickers this year, never seen such a fast group. They're going to get you to market just that much faster."

Camden stuck his finger in his ear and wiggled it as though he were clearing an obstruction. Pop was looking back at him in a silent face-off.

I broke the silence again. "I think we're going to have to harvest again in a few more weeks. Quite a few of the oranges will be ripe for picking then. In a few months those orange blossoms are going to be replaced by fruit."

Camden tapped the side of his shoes with his cane, knocking loose orange dust and mud from the bottom.

"What's wrong with the old man?" he said slowly, deliberately, almost like he was recovering from a partial stroke. His head was turned away from Pop.

"He's been feeling a little under the weather."

"Is that a medical description? I thought you were a doctor."

"I am." I looked at my father. Although I couldn't see his eyes, I knew he could hear me. "He'll be fine."

"Well, all right then."

Camden hobbled back toward his house and opened the gate. He was leaning to one side. I drifted back into the truck and waited for Pop to blast me.

"What did that old cracker ask you about me?"

I answered, "Just how you're doing?"

"Why is he asking about me? We're not friends."

"I guess he was being neighborly. I don't know why you're surprised, Pop. You two have known each other for over forty years. It was a nice gesture."

"He's just trying to find out when I'm going to die. Hell, I think he's held on this long because he wants me to die first."

"Why would you think that?" I asked.

"Long story. I don't have time to go into it. Camden Murphy doesn't have to worry. I'm gonna die first just so I can get Hell ready for him by turning up the heat."

"I don't think he feels that way, Pop."

"You don't know him like I do, but he's goin' to his grave with that guilt. These lips will never say, 'I forgive you.' "

"Are you ever going to tell me what happened between the two of you?"

"Why? It doesn't concern you. I made it right years ago. When we die, it will be all over."

"Pop, how does he know that I'm a doctor?"

"There are no secrets around here. People just don't want to talk about what they know."

Camden Murphy's house looked no different than it did when I was a boy. As children, my brother and I weren't allowed to play in the yard. The furthest we could go was to the edge of the grove, sometimes to the plant, but Mathew would break the rule all the time. He'd disappear for hours. Come to think of it so did John, Camden's oldest child.

They'd play tag for hours in the grove and nobody was the wiser. Mathew spent most of his time with John, instead of me, looking for adventure on the acreage or in the plant. Pop constantly reminded Mat to remember his role. He'd say, "Mathew, if you need somebody to play with, play with your brother. Folks 'round here don't care for colored boys keepin' company with white boys. It shouldn't make a difference, but it does." Mathew would nod his head and be off with John minutes later.

I drove slowly back to Pop's house remembering little pieces of history on the way. "Pop, how many children did Camden and Adelaide have?"

He shifted in his seat as though sitting on a small rock. His discomfort was obvious. He looked out the window, trying to avoid eye contact, but I waited patiently for his response. "Three," he reluctantly said.

"John died right around the same time that Mathew died. I don't know if I remembered or if Momma told me. Terri's still kicking around here. Who is the other one, and where is he or she?

"Mind your business. Don't go stirring up ghosts."

"It was a boy, wasn't it?"

"I guess so."

"Well, what happened to him?"

"I *think* he drowned."

"Drowned where?" I asked.

"In the lake," he replied.

"Which lake?"

Pop snapped, "How many lakes do we have around here?"

"There's only one that I know of."

"Okay, then that's the one. Leave it alone, Kenny. Let it go."

"What was his name?"

"His name was Miller."

"Like the beer?"

"Exactly. Hurry it up. I need to use the john. By the way, you need to stop at Reilly's Pharmacy. I'm nearly out of tonic."

"Not a problem. So how old was Miller when he died?"

"Can't say I know for sure. Younger than the girl, I think."

"Terri?"

"Yeah."

"How'd he end up in the lake?"

"Hell if I know. I'm not his father and he's not my son. How come you don't ask all them questions about Mathew? He's your business. We got a lifetime of things to think about in our own family. Why do you insist on goin' into another dog's yard?"

"Don't know, Pop. I just started remembering things after I saw the house. It's been a long time."

"You think Terri is in there askin' her father about Mathew? Do you? I don't thinks so. She got good enough sense to worry about her own people."

"What's that suppose to mean?"

"There are plenty of colored folk, good people, whose children disappeared. Who's worryin' 'bout them? Nobody, that's who. You spendin' all this time worryin' about one white kid when you oughtta be thinkin' about all the colored people that's been strung up in the woods then burnt 'til nothin' but fertilizer was left. That's what you should be thinkin' about."

"It was just a question."

"Some questions are better left unasked. Like I said, just leave it be."

"I'm a Murphy," I said. "When have we ever been able to leave anything alone? That's what being a Murphy is all about, isn't it?" I smiled but he didn't.

"I've said all I'm gonna say, Kenny."

The questions made the drive home long for Pop and short for me. Before I knew it, we were back, parked neatly on the side of the house. I left the engine running while Pop got out.

"You need anything else from the store?" I asked Pop. "May as well pick up a few things while I'm there."

Chapter 9

The Rainbow Food Market was nearly empty. The floor looked barely walked on. The shelves were filled to the edge and every item was squared to the lip. Soft country music was piped through the public address system, mostly Waylon Jennings and Randy Travis.

I walked the aisle searching for a few simple items: capers, artichokes, and sesame seed oil. After two days, I was tired of soul food. I couldn't find any items on my A list. The information counter seemed a logical place to go. The young woman behind the desk was puzzled by my request and scurried off down aisle 9 and 10, sure that if the market stocked any of my items, they'd be on one of the two ethnic food aisles. I waited patiently, but she came back empty handed. The only words she understood were "seed" and "oil."

"Teriyaki sauce. Do you have Teriyaki sauce?"

"If we have it, it would be on aisle six near the barbecue sauce." The girls sounded like Reba McIntyre.

Aisle six was a long way away to be disappointed. Sure enough, the barbecue sauces were there, stocked from floor to ceiling. Every brand was available including some home-grown varieties, including Uncle Lester's Down-home Grillin sauce. There was, however, no Teriyaki sauce.

Disappointed, I headed for the exit and down to Reilly's, thinking that at least I could get tonic for Pop. I pushed open the door and stepped up to the prescription counter where Mr. Clark sat at the window. "A bottle of Doc John's," I said.

Mr. Clark answered. "It's all gone. I don't know if we'll be getting any more. It seems that Dr. John's has gone out of business. The distributor said that the DEA wanted to know where the manufacturer was getting the secret ingredient used in the tonic."

"What ingredient is that?"

"I don't know," groaned Mr. Clark. If I knew that, it wouldn't be a secret—would it?"

"I just need one more bottle for my Pop. You've got to have another bottle somewhere back there. He's just starting to feel better."

"Sold the last three bottles a few minutes ago. Sorry, that's all she wrote."

"Terri?"

"Yup. If you run, you may be able to catch her. She left here no more'n five minutes ago. She might sell you a bottle."

I dashed through the door. Terri was across the street, standing at the door of the company truck. Her hands were full. She juggled the bags while trying to pull the keys from her purse. She found the key ring but struggled to find the key to the Ford. I approached with cautious confidence.

"May I help you with your bag, Ms. Murphy?"

"Go screw yourself," she said.

"Only if you watch."

I eased up to her, taking the keys from her hands. "You might want to read the next time. It's easier that way. The one that works for this lock is the one labeled F-o-r-d." I opened the lock and pulled the door. Terri slid the bag onto the floor on the passenger side before gesturing for the return of her property.

"What do you want?" she asked as if she and I had just broken up.

"Just a bottle of tonic. I'm willing to pay," I said.

"Are you? Mr. Clark told you that I bought the last three bottles, huh?"

"Sure did. My Daddy's feelin' a might poorly and good ol' Doc John's always perks him up. He's just about out. Sure would appreciate the help, Miss." My Amos and Andy impression did nothing to loosen her grip on those liquid treasures.

"Not my problem. These are for Mr. Camden Murphy, sole proprietor of Murphy's Orange Grove."

"I said I'd pay you."

"How much you got," she asked. "Better yet, what is one of these gems worth to you?"

Her breast mounds looked so round and full. They were like good-sized grapefruit. "*Mmmm*, what do you want for them? The tonic—I'm talking about the tonic." She noticed me admiring her breasts.

Terri drove a hard bargain. "I'll sell you one bottle for $200."

"Go screw yourself!"

"Only if *you* watch," she countered. "Seems to me like a big, important doctor like you shouldn't have a problem with $200. Unless of course that fake Murphy daddy of yours isn't worth it."

"I'll give you fifty bucks and a promise that I won't tell your Daddy that you keep offering to screw me. Will that work?"

"Only in your dreams, Mister. The price is going up. Now we're up to $250." Terri started the truck engine and put it into gear. "Going once, going twice . . ."

"Just wait a minute. Be reasonable. $60 gives you nearly a forty-dollar profit."

"So what. The law of supply and demand says that I can get more. Going thrice . . ."

"Okay." I opened my wallet and counted out $200 dollars and then shoved it back into my pocket. "How do I know you'll give me the tonic once I pay you."

"Trust," she said.

"I can't trust you."

"Why not? Our fathers did almost forty years of business on trust. I will respect my father's reputation if you will respect yours."

"All right," I said. I reached down in my pocket for the wad of bills. I handed it to her and she pushed it down into her purse. She leaned over and pulled a single bottle of tonic from the wrinkled brown bag and handed it to me."

She laughed as she sped off into the evening. I had a bottle of tonic and she had about thirty dollars, thanks to a trick I learned in college. "Stupid, white girl," I said aloud. "I wonder how long it's going to take her to figure it out."

Not long. I felt a solid shot to the rear bumper of Pop's truck. My head crashed into the steering wheel. A glance in my rearview mirror told me that Crazy Terri was backing up to ram me again. I fired up the truck, put it into gear, and begged the eight-cylinder Chevy to give me the best it had. Terri missed me by inches. I did a 180 and pulled along side her.

I yelled at her through my open passenger side window. "You crazy heifer. Are you off your medication or something?"

"I want my tonic back," she said. "That's what I get for trying to cut a square deal with a phony." Terri wadded up the money in her hands and tossed it at me. A gust of wind blew the cash away from my passenger side window. "There's nothing honest about you people, is there?"

I gunned it before she got any new ideas. The tires squealed as I peeled off. I tried to lose her by weaving off the dirt road separating Murphy's Grove from Pop's house. She knew the area better than I did, but a navigational mistake wrecked the front-end of her daddy's pick up truck.

I walked to the driver's side window and watched as Terri banged her head against the air bag and pounded her fist against the dashboard. She cursed like a call girl with the claps. "You okay?" I asked

"You stupid bastard. Do I look all right to you?"

"Actually you do, but I don't think those bottles are going to make it." Terri looked down on the floor of the cab. Liquid from two broken bottles pooled on the plastic floor mat. Shards of broken glass jutted upward from the surface of the expanding circle.

"You made me do this. I hate you!" Terri was red.

"You cheated me first. It's not my fault that you can't drive. I opened the door of the cab. "I don't think you should stay in there. There's no telling what's in those bottles."

Terri slammed the door. "What am I going to tell my father? This was his favorite truck."

"Try 'I'm sorry and I'll have it fixed.'" Easiness softened her face. She threw up her hands and plopped down on the dirt road, shaking her head.

I offered my help. "Let me give you a ride. It's dark you shouldn't be out here alone."

"You're not too bright—are you? I should have known that, seeing as how you went to one of those Affirmative Action schools."

"Now you're being caddy. Forget it, you can walk."

"Is that one of those fancy college words? So, you're dumb *and* you have no sense of direction. The grove is less than a quarter mile from here," Terri said.

"5000 feet or five inches don't make a bit of difference to me. You're still walking."

"Did I bruise the monkey's feelings? Poor thing. I got bananas to make you feel better."

I stopped in my tracks. She'd gotten to me. "No, I'm no ordinary monkey. I'm King Kong." I grabbed my crotch in a boyish gesture. "Here's your banana right here. Where should I put it?"

Short silence followed. Terri started first. She couldn't hold back the crack of laughter. It was contagious. Before we knew it, we were giddy.

"At least I have the last bottle of Tonic," she said.

"Says who? Last I remember you sold it for thirty dollars."

"I gave you your money back," she replied.

"No, you threw *your* money to the wind. If you're really nice to me, I'll share the bottle with you."

"How're we going to do that?" she asked.

"I can top off my father's bottle then bring you the rest."

"Why don't I fill my Daddy's bottle and bring *you* the rest," Terri countered.

"What happened to trust?" I asked.

"Trust was broken with those other bottles."

I drove her to the edge of the tall grass leading to the grove and turned off the lights of Pop's Chevy. "This is your stop," I said.

"Yeah, thanks Kenneth."

She'd never called my name before. It was music to me. There was a long pause before she bumped the door open. I wanted to fill that uncomfortable silence with a memory.

"Terri? Have you ever . . ."

Somehow she understood the unfinished question. "Yes, I have—at school—it was like, wow!"

Then she was gone, and I remained, unable to move, unable to think. I replayed the tape in mind. Did she really understand? Did I? I cranked the engine and drove the quarter-mile to the house. I wasn't feeling well. Pop had already diagnosed me. I had a bad case of white girl fever.

As soon as I arrived "Where you been?" greeted me through the open door of the back porch.

"Just around. I got the last bottle of tonic. There won't be anymore after this."

"I won't need anymore than that, son."

Chapter 10

Pop and I awoke early the next morning. It seemed that neither one of us got much sleep the night before.

"What are you doing, Pop?"

"Just thinking."

"About what?"

"The way things could've been."

Pop had that far away look in his eyes. I'd seen it other people, people whose essence was evaporating like the morning dew, those people who'd already let go and were simply waiting for wings. I looked closer and saw that my father still had one hand on life. He wouldn't leave until he finished his work. He had things to do. He knew it and I knew it too.

"Beautiful morning, isn't it?" I asked

"How can you tell?"

"Can't you smell the gardenias and honeysuckle?"

"That don't tell me a thing. It's like that most mornin's," he said pessimistically.

I inhaled a lung full. "I don't get this in the city."

Pop ruined the moment. "Don't get too comfortable. You've already overstayed your welcome."

"Why is that?" I asked for the fiftieth time.

"'Cause what you're really sayin' is that you startin' to like it here. That tells me you gettin' too comfortable—Ocala's suckin' you in—like I told you it would."

"No, it's not."

"I'm not gonna argue with you, but I can see it all over you. This place is no place for you—I tell you."

"I can handle myself, Pop."

"You better, 'cause this place is just like a good bar: you're always leavin' but you never left."

"That might be true for other people who live around here, but not to me. Ocala's too slow. I need the excitement of the big city."

"Get goin', then. No use in wastin' more time." After a brief moment of reflection, he said, "Come inside. I want to show you somethin'."

"Show me what?"

"Hush, boy, and follow me."

Pop walked me through the kitchen and into the bedroom he shared with Momma. Her favorite lavender hat was still perched on the nightstand. He dropped to his knees to get a box from under the bed. It was tightly wrapped with cord.

"You see this box?"

"Yes."

"There are important things inside. I'm gonna give it to you now, but don't open it until I die. Promise."

Curiosity overpowered commitment. "What's in it?" I said.

"I said promise, boy!"

"I promise."

"This box has been in our family for three generations. You are my only son and when I die, what's in it will be yours."

"Okay, but what's in it?"

"Your history and my honor. When my momma gave it to me, she told me to be still for ninety days after openin' it; I'm tellin' you the same thing."

"Okay, but why?"

Pop was still speaking in riddles. "What's in this box could make you do something stupid, that's why."

"I understand," I said but I really didn't. I had no stomach for this kind of *Color Purple* shit.

"I've added things to the box, some of my things some of your momma's. When you have a child, you do the same. Look at me, boy! What I'm sayin' is important."

Pop reverently handed the box to me, the way the deacons handle communion. He put it in my hand and then put his hands on top of mine.

"Son, the whole Murphy stake is in this box."

The moment was interrupted by a hard knock at the door. Before answering, I put away the box and my immediate curiosity. "Do you want me to get the door?"

We both peeped through the living room curtain and saw a Murphy's Grove truck drive up to the front door. It looked like Terri, and someone else was riding in the passenger seat.

"You get it, Kenneth. I don't have time to play with that child."

I unlocked the front door. It was Terri. I was happy to see her, but didn't know why she'd come.

"Ms. Murphy," I said in a business tone. She cut me off, quick.

"You know why I'm here. Give it to me," she demanded. I'd forgotten about the deal we struck to split the tonic.

Pop sat on the back porch. The door and windows were open. From the front door, I couldn't tell if he was listening.

"Just a moment," I said and walked toward the bathroom and the medicine chest where I put the unopened bottle of tonic next to the half empty one.

Terri spoke from the door in a less than discreet voice. "Hurry up, I don't have all day," she said through the screen.

I hurried before Pop got wind of what we were doing. I grabbed the half-empty bottle, rushed back to the front door, and placed the bottle in her hands. "Is there anything else?" I asked monotonously.

"Yes. You need to check the workers. They're starting to pick the young oranges again."

"I'll be there in a few minutes." I closed the door and rushed back to where Pop had been sitting. He was already gone. "Pop," I called out. "Where are you?"

As I walked back to the front of the house, I saw the top of Pop's head moving past the window on the side of the house. When he appeared in the front yard, Pop hung his head so that he could see who else was in the Murphy truck. It was a man who I didn't recognize, but Pop did. Pop pulled his 45-caliber military issue and fired two quick shots into the ground.

"What you do that for?" I asked.

"I told that cracker that if he ever stepped foot on my property, he was a dead man. Now *that* was a warning shot. The next one I'm gonna put in his head."

Terri put the truck into gear and drove off.

"Who are you talking about, Pop?"

"Kennelly. Dublin Kennelly. He's the foreman of the processing plant. I should have killed him years ago. I would have, too, if I didn't have to worry about you and your Momma."

"What did he do?"

"He killed my son. Mathew and your momma are dead because of him." Pop walked to the back of the house and I followed him. He put the pistol under a bucket near the porch.

"How did he kill Mathew?" There was a long silence before he spoke.

"Forget about it, but never forget that crackers killed your brother and your mother."

"I'm confused," I said.

"Never mind, son" he said and walked the path to the woods.

"I'm coming with you," I said.

"No!"

"Okay, then I'm leaving for a few minutes to check on the workers. We have to stay on top of them."

Pop stopped cold in his tracks. "We? *We* are not in the business, *I* am. Go on back to

Lauderdale. This is the last time I'm gonna tell you this. You're not in the orange business!"

I went through the front door and into the bright morning sun. I started the truck and drove over to the grove. When I arrived, I checked basket after basket of oranges. Not one orange was too young for harvest.

I inspected the last of the baskets near the processing plant. Terri saw me and came out of the office. Through the large plate glass window, I could see the top of Camden's head rocking back in forth.

"Terri, I thought you said the workers were picking unripe oranges. I checked them all. They're fine."

Terri had a twinkle in her eye. "Let me show you what your workers are doing. Follow me."

Terri walked into the processing plant to the sorters. She picked one of the oranges from the washing troughs and sliced it open with a pocketknife.

"Taste," she said as she handed me half.

The orange was exactly as I expected it to be.

"And?" I asked.

"Is that sweet, full, and ripe?" she asked

"Yes." I said emphatically.

"How about these?" Terri lifted her shirt and showed me her pink grapefruits. "Taste them," she said with an impish grin. I did.

She pulled my head into her fruit basket, stroking the back of my head and neck. Then, she held my face in both her hands and began to lick me like a toffee lollipop, gently then more aggressively. "You are delicious," she cooed.

It was just like I imagined it would be, but my father's voice echoed in my head. His words woke me from my short indulgence. "We can't do this," I said, more to convince myself than to stop her.

"*Ssshhh*," she whispered. "This is what I want."

I felt trapped between cities. What was wrong in Ocala was right in Fort Lauderdale. My mind raced in search of an excuse, any excuse, to let this continue. *Kenneth, they're not like us. Kenneth, crackers killed your brother and your Momma.* It played in my head like a scratched 45 on an old turntable.

"No," my mouth said, as I unzipped her jeans and reached in to touch. "We can't . . .."

She responded with breathy sighs. Every moan and groan was a synonym for yes. We were saved by the *bam* of the heavy metal door and *hiss* of steam being released from the orange press.

I waited nervously for the second slam to tell me that whoever was there was gone. After the second slam came, I bolted from the processing plant. I reached into my pocket and slid my manhood back to its resting place, just in case Camden found me. I didn't know where Terri went or what she did to fix herself so quickly, but before I could put the transmission into gear, she handed me a note. *Meet me by the lake tonight at nine.* I drove off without saying a word.

Thoughts of Terri made my head spin while I drove to Pop's. I pulled the truck up to the front door and walked inside, still tingling from a few sips of Terri's juice.

"Why did you park the truck at the front door?" Pop asked, Yoda-like. I already knew that his question was not about the truck. He knew something.

"I'll go move it."

"What did Camden's daughter want?"

"Nothing really."

"Be a man," he commanded.

"What's that suppose to mean?" I wore guilt like a tight suit. There was no hiding it from him. I had been with a white woman.

"If you want a white woman, be man enough to say so."

"I don't want a white woman or any woman right now. I'm just trying to take care of some business."

"Sit down, son. We need to talk."

Pop looked frail again. He was slipping away and he knew it. The sicker he became, the more he wanted to talk. He had secrets that he needed to tell. Over the last few days he had talked to me more than he had during my entire life. It was his chance at confession and I was his reluctant priest.

"Remember when you were picking colleges to go to?"

"Yes," I said while waiting for the figurative shoe to drop.

"And, you wanted to go to that school in California. Broccoli, I think it was called."

"Berkeley."

"You got in, didn't you?"

"Yes."

"Why didn't you go there instead of Florida A&M?"

"Momma said that she didn't want me around strangers so far away from home."

"Is that all you remember?"

"Pretty much."

"Your mother had a gentle spirit about her, but the truth was harder than that. I didn't want you to go to a white school. I didn't think they could make a man of you the way a black school could. No white school could prepare you for what you'd face as a colored man. It was a hard decision."

"I can appreciate what your saying, but where are you going with this?" I hurriedly asked

"Just hold your horses. I'm gettin' there as fast as this old mind can take me."

It was getting late and I wanted to be at the lake to meet Terri.

"What's the point, Pop?"

"You in a rush or somethin'? . . . So, like I was sayin' . . ."

"—Can we talk about this later. I've got to make a few important calls to Lauderdale. "

"Okay, but we got to finish this conversation."

"Thanks." I got up from the porch to move the truck and take a shower. Pop was staring into the woods again. I thought he was finished with me, but he wasn't.

"So, where're you takin' her?"

"Taking who?"

"Mixed couples aren't welcomed much around here, Kenny. There ain't many places you two can go. But you're grown. Do what you want. Just be ready to pay the piper," he said.

Fear should have loosened lust's hold on me. Are you okay with this?" I asked.

"Nope, I'm still your father. I don't haveta agree with nothin' you do—'specially when I know you headin' for trouble."

"We're just going to talk."

"Uh-huh, talk. It wasn't that long ago when talkin' to a white girl would get you a rope necklace and a spot up a tree. Still happens out here every once in awhile. They just got smarter about it, that's all."

"How did you know I was meeting Terri?"

"She's never been here before. I knew she wanted somethin' or maybe somebody. Damn sure not me. All the time we've been doin' business, we always met in the grove. I'm old, but stupid I'm not. You be careful, son."

"Like I said, we're just going to talk."

"You know how I feel, don't you, boy? Race mixin' has never turned into nothin' good. You ought to know that from marryin' that girl, and she ain't but one-quarter white. Look how much trouble she caused you."

"That's different."

"Different how?" he asked.

"*Damn*, Pop, I SAID we're just going to talk."

"Watch your tone, boy! See what I'm sayin', she's already got you disrespectin' your momma."

"How am I disrespecting Momma?"

Pop pointed to the truck. "See where you parked?" The truck nearly blocked the front staircase. "Now you know how your Momma felt about that. This is still, and will forever be, your Momma's home. Don't you ever forget it!"

What could I say? He was right.

Chapter 11

We were to meet at the lake at nine, but I arrived early enough to feed my curiosity and settle my nerves. I opened the window to take in the sights and sounds, but it was the smell that got my attention. I took a deep breath and realized the scent was somehow familiar. I recognized it as the scent of distrust.

I'd left the light on in my truck—Pop's truck, I mean, as a beacon for Terri but also to comfort me in the darkness, a solitary black man out in the woods, steeped in unnatural stillness. It was as though Mother Nature held her breath.

Lake Seminola was hallowed ground to all Ocalans; at least it used to be, so I should have felt none of the uneasiness that was working its way through my veins. It was the only place in the county where peace reigned, where for a time wolf and sheep put away conflict, each by controlling its own form of fear. It was a fitting place for Terri and me to come together.

The approaching van sounded like a large beast lumbering through the woods. Except for the squeak of Terri's parking brake, it was unusually quiet and still for a place that should have been teeming with life. I stepped out of the truck to listen for other sounds, the sounds of life. I heard none. A cautious hello from Terri was a welcomed distraction.

At the shoreline, the lights from Terri's van bounced off the tiny surface ripples on the lake and then skipped to the distant edge where the large white intake pipes siphoned water into the bulky filtration machinery. It was a disturbing sight for me, who in my childhood drank directly from the lake. Then the lake shimmered and sparkled sapphire blue. Since, filth had corrupted the lake, and its power to bring people together was undone.

Terri got out of the van and stood next to me. Her hair was blowing freely in the August breeze. The headlamps cast our shadows onto the water. Our silhouettes told nothing about our backgrounds. It was just the outline of a man and a woman standing together on the bank of Lake Seminola.

"When I was small, we weren't allowed to come here," Terri said.

I remained fixated on the stillness of the waters.

"The colored people would come here by the dozens to fish. Sometimes Daddy would buy the extras, but most of the time, he and Uncle Paul would go to a place where white people gathered to fish," she said.

"Who decided where blacks could fish and where whites could fish?"

"Don't know; it's just always been that way."

I tucked my hands into the pockets of my blue jeans. I wasn't cold. It was just comforting to do so.

"White people around here mostly fish in the river further north.

"Why is that? The fishing was good in the lake."

"Well, I guess they didn't want to be near the colored people. Uncle Paul said the fish in the river were healthier because they had to swim against the current and the water had more air in it.

"That's funny because that's why the black people won't drink lake water. Anything that goes into the lake stays in the lake. There is no way for the lake to clean itself. My daddy still won't drink from the lake.

Terri said, "Kennelly said that the lake water is the safest water to drink because colored folks would never do anything to the water because they eat the fish from it."

"*African-American*, Terri."

"I'm sorry. *African-American.* Didn't you just call them black? Is there a difference? I think your people have changed what they call themselves three times in the last ten years. If you can't keep up, how do you expect us to keep up?" Terri asked.

"It's a matter of choice, perspective, and sensitivity. Black people are trying to define themselves."

"How about you? Are you trying to define yourself?"

"Never really thought about it," I said

"Think about it now. I'm curious."

"I guess I consider myself a man first, then a black man."

"Where does *doctor* fit in your description?" she asked. I never imagined that she could be so thoughtful. Her interest in me was intoxicating.

"That's part of who I am too," I answered.

"I would think it's more of what you do," Terri said to correct me."

"It depends," I said.

"On what?"

"I think over the years what I do became part of who I am. At this point, those two sides make me who I am."

"Even when you're dealing with your father?"

"Well, parents are parents. No matter how we mature, their impression of us never changes."

Terri crossed her arms over her chest and pulled her shoulders to her ears.

"Cold?" I asked.

"Just a little. I have a blanket in the van."

"Why don't we just get in the van?" Terri and I were not on a date, so I wasn't going to open her door. This was business. We had business to discuss. Yeah, business.

Once inside, Terri reached over and turned on the radio. Surprisingly, she skipped the country station and found one that played middle-of-the-road pop.

"Is this all right?" she asked.

"That's fine, but I prefer adult contemporary or jazz."

"Me too. I mean rock and metal are okay. But I like mellow stuff. Do you like funk and hip-hop?"

"Some of it is okay, but I like music that brightens my spirit. Why did you ask me to meet you?" I asked abruptly.

"Because we need an understanding if we are going to work together. Neither one of our fathers is in good health. It won't be long before you and I are making all of the decisions. I'd like to have an understanding before that day comes. Lots of people are depending on us to make this work."

"I'm listening."

"That doesn't make sense to you?" she asked in disbelief of my cavalier attitude.

"Of course it does," I said.

"We need each other because both our families make money from the grove."

"True," I said. "But I think it's a little early to be planning takeover."

"I just think we could have a better working relationship than our fathers," she said

"I agree, but I may sell the business after my father dies. That's what he wants me to do."

Terri focused on my face. "I guess you like living in the city too, huh?"

"That's where my practice and home are. The city has become my element. I feel a little out of place here."

"You don't think *I* came back here by choice—do you? My father is sick, too, and I am all he has left."

"What about Kennelly?" I asked.

"What about him? He works for Murphy's Grove, nothing more, and I don't trust him."

"Why not, Terri?"

"My mother, God bless the dead, didn't like him. She swore until the day she died that Kennelly was partly to blame for my brother's death."

"Which brother?"

"John. Miller drowned in this lake."

"How'd that happen?" I asked pulling a mint from my pocket.

"I don't know all the details. I was very young. Miller was maybe four or so when he died. I was around six and John would have been around ten if he were alive then."

"Your mother lost two sons and you lost two brothers. It must be tough. Losing Mathew was hard on my whole family."

"I was a child, Kenny. I don't think I got the full impact of their deaths. To me they just went away. Daddy still talks about them on occasion. Some times he sits teary-eyed for hours staring at our last family picture.

"Miller," I said to Terri who was lost in her own thoughts. "You were telling me about your little brother, Miller."

"Nothing more to tell. He was found floating in this lake. They think he followed somebody and then slipped in and drowned."

"Not much time between tragedies, huh?"

"No, not much," she answered. "This is another reason for us to make the peace that our fathers didn't. Murphy's Grove is a special place for both our families."

"I know."

"Do you really? The same accident killed both our brothers. You lost Mathew; we lost John," she said

"Luke, if everybody wasn't so against race mixing, I think our families would have been much closer, especially after the accident."

"Why'd you call me Luke?"

Nobody outside of the family knew that Luke was Momma's pet name for me. She started calling me that after Mathew died. Nobody, not even Daddy, had called me that since. It was Momma's special name for me.

"My Momma called you Luke."

"Your Momma? Your Momma never spoke a word to me my whole life."

"Kenneth Luke is what she mostly called you. Daddy called you Carnell's youngest boy."

"Your family had time to keep up with mine? That's strange. We never talked about the white Murphys in our house. That was my father's doing. He said that our connection with your family was business only."

"Maybe that's all it was to Carnell. If you say that I told you this, I'll call you a bald-face liar."

"What?" I asked, sitting on the edge of my seat.

" . . . Daddy asks me about Carnell every day."

"Why is that?"

"You gotta be kidding me, right?" Terri asked incredulously.

"No, I'm not."

"If you had a business partner for more than forty years, wouldn't you care?"

"Depends," I replied.

"Depends on what?"

"What kind of business relationship we had. It's not like they're friends," I answered.

"Why because they didn't say it, or eat at each other's house? You can't really be that stupid. Think about the times."

"That's still no reason for Camden to take advantage of my father. Pop was working for peanuts for years."

"Damn, you *are* that stupid. Labor was as easy as oranges to find around here. You don't think my father couldn't have put together his own team of workers? He threw business to your father and he's still doing it."

"You're not going to make me believe that. There are always two sides to a story," I countered.

"My father owns the grove. Don't you think people have come to ask my father if they can work for him during harvest season? My father tells all of them that they need to talk to Carnell if they want a job."

"So your father is Mr. Nice Guy. I suppose he wasn't getting anything out of it, huh?"

"Like what, Kenneth?"

"My father took the headache of managing the labor and handling quality control before the oranges got to the processing plant."

"Listen to yourself. It's pathetic. Think about what you just said and ask yourself if Kennelly couldn't have produced the same results. The man has been on our payroll for decades, for God's sake."

"I still don't buy the philanthropy crap. Camden Murphy is a businessman and has always been one. He doesn't know any other way." Our conversation was turning into a debate. "I got to go."

"Go? I thought we were just getting started," she said.

"Another time, Terri."

I drove home in a hurry but Pop was already sleeping. He had Momma's picture resting on his chest. I blew out the kerosene lamp and went to bed. The questions floating in my head gave me little rest during the night.

Chapter 12

Pop was up his usual time, 5 a.m. I refused to get up until my bladder forced me to the bathroom. After I was up and empty, I drove myself toward the coffee pot. I was tired, dog tired, from a night filled with more answers than questions.

"Coffee's ready," Pop said as I passed him, bare-chest, in the kitchen.

"Thanks."

Pop stared at my naked chest in disgust. "Do you need to wash clothes?"

I knew what he was talking about but didn't give him an answer. I just sat down across from him with a hot cup of coffee, tapping my fingers and stroking my forehead.

"Somethin' on your mind?" I asked.

"Guess you could say that," he answered.

Pop pushed his chair away from the table and walked the short distance to the stove to pour another cup. "I'm on the porch," he said.

The porch was his place of power. I didn't want to go out there. It was either a trap or an escape, depending on the circumstances. If I asked just the wrong question, he'd run into the woods, so I stood in the doorway of the back porch, sizing up my options, planning my approach.

"How exactly did Mathew die?"

He banged his seldom-used pipe on the doorjamb to loosen the ashes inside. "That white girl done stirred you up, huh? Well, what did she tell you?"

"She said that my brother and her brother died in the same accident."

"That's partly true. She was small then. She probably don't remember the whole story. Then again, maybe she do and only told you what she wants you to know."

Pop was being coy, trying to throw me off with innuendo, but I didn't fall for it. "Pop, I didn't ask you about her story or yours. I just want to hear about what happened to Mathew."

"He died."

"Tell me more," I insisted.

"He didn't have to, but he did. Mat fell from a good height onto a metal pole. Tore clear through to his liver."

"There's more, much more, and you know what it is."

"Remember we were supposed to finish our conversation about Florida A & M University."

"What does that have to do with Mathew's death?"

"If you just sit down and listen, Kenny, you'll understand. By the way, when are you goin' back to Lauderdale. I'm probably as well as I'm gonna be before I die."

"You're changing the subject again, Pop. I wanted to hear your version of the story. I could see Terri tonight and she'd tell me anything I want to know. Is that what you want?"

"That's your decision, but you won't get the right story. If she tells you, what you'll hear is that nothing could have helped my boy. In their story, I'm the villain; her father is the hero."

Pop changed his focus again before I could ask another question.

"So anyway, FAMU," he said. "We wanted you to be educated so we sent you there to learn what's in those books but a whole lot more about what's not in those books—life stuff."

"Okay," I said waiting for a revelation or at least a link between Mathew and FAMU. "Go on."

"We wanted you close just in case you had to come home and takeover the business.

"Why would I have had to come home?"

"That's not the point," Pop said," just listen."

"Well, what is the point?"

"It was a good school and all, but your Momma and I thought that I might not be around."

"Why is that?"

"Some white folks came callin' one day, sayin' that I had somethin' to do with Miller's death."

"Why?"

"Why do you think?" he asked.

"I don't know, that's why I'm asking."

"Because I'm colored," he said.

"*African-American*."

"I'm no African. I was born right here. And, I don't want to hear that foolishness about me bein' black, cause I'm not, I'm brown, light brown. I'm colored."

"All right, all right, just finish the story!"

"I told you 'bout rushin' me, boy. Anyway, white folk around here always believed that a *colored* had somethin' to do with that boy's drownin'. Years after it happened, they framed some black boy on the northeast side of town. They scared him so bad that he told them that a man who lived near the lake killed that boy. Nobody lives closer to the lake than me."

"Who did he say killed Miller?"

"Are you really that dumb? He's talkin' about me, who else?"

"Did you?" I asked after a dead silence.

"No, I didn't kill him. I could have, but I didn't."

"What do you mean by that?"

"It would have been justice. Camden let your brother die. Truth be told, I didn't care too much for that boy Miller. He was Kennelly's favorite. I heard Kennelly teaching him to hate and that boy was a natural."

"I'm confused, Pop. Over the last three days, the only person, according to you, who was not responsible for Mathew's death is me. You better lay off the tonic."

"Don't be funny, boy. I say it like I see it. Crackers killed my boy. That's the way it is."

Pop moved to the edge of the porch like he always did just before walking into the woods. He put one foot on the first rung of the stairs and then the other foot. He stepped down two of the five stairs and then stopped suddenly.

"When are you going to stop running? I asked. 'A man is not what he says, but what he does'—who taught me that?"

My words froze Pop in his steps. It seemed like an eternity. He pivoted and climbed slowly back up the stairs, crossing his arms over his chest before stepping onto the landing.

"When are you leavin'?" he asked.

"I'm not leaving until you're better, coming with me, or dead. Make your choice."

"You're goin' home then. I'll tell you what you want to know. Pop's eyes were wide and fixed as he began to tell what he knew, or what he imagined. It really didn't matter though because it was real to him.

****

What did they know? John and Mathew were lively nine-year-old boys. They lived in the world inside the grove's fence, where boys could be boys and people could be people.

I remember the first time they met. That little devil walked right up to my Mathew and licked his face. The boys must have been around two then. Camden saw John put his tongue on Mathew and snatched him by the collar. When he asked John why he licked Mathew, John said, "I wanted to taste the chocolate." Camden and I both had a good laugh. From then on, wherever you saw one of the boys, you could bet your eyetooth that the other was close behind. I used to call them Blackman and Robber like Batman and Robin 'cause of all the trouble those two would get into.

John ran into the processing plant where the oranges were washed in big troughs. The good oranges were bagged and tagged. The dented or dinged oranges were juiced by a huge press, turned to concentrate and pasteurized before being sold to Tropicana.

Restless John wanted a new challenge every day. "Let's play Tarzan. We'll use those pipes and swing over the press," dared John.

Mathew didn't like his chances as he looked at the thin pipe, twenty-five to thirty feet up. "Suppose we fall in?"

"We won't fall. I've done it before. You're not scared are you?" asked John.

"Nope. I ain't afraid of nothin'!" Mathew pushed the ladder up the wall and with John's help moved it to a spot underneath the horizontal pipe. "I'll go first," Mathew said as he climbed up the ladder and reached for the pipe with one hand. He was hanging by one hand like a trapeze artist. Mathew moved toward the huge vat.

"Mathew, I tricked you. I've never been up there. Got to admit that it looks awful scary from down here . . . but if you can do it, I can too."

John put his foot on the bottom rung of the ladder and prepared himself to climb.

"It's easy. Come on." Mathew dangled from the pipes while talkin' to John. He told me he could've stayed hangin' there all day if it weren't for that red-faced drunk, Dublin Kennelly.

"Get down from there you little ape!" Kennelly's boomin' voice loosened Mathew's grip. My boy fell thirty feet to the floor. Mathew hit his face on his bent knee and knocked out a bottom tooth in addition to bustin' his lip. "Good for ya. Now git before I string ya up there permanently."

Mathew ran out and into the grove to get away from Kennelly. John was much slower and got caught by his collar. Bad enough that he'd been caught, but he had to hear Kennelly's trash talkin' the whole way to Camden's office.

"Do you want your baby brother playing with niggers, too?" Miller peeped out from his makeshift clubhouse under Kennelly's desk. "If you were my son, I scorch your backside," Kennelly told John, unaware that Miller was under the desk.

Camden was in his office when Kennelly came in, draggin' John by the collar.

"Murphy. Murphy, I found your boy getting ready to swing on the pipes over the press. He was followin' that baby gorilla."

"What Gorilla?"

"Carnell's boy."

"Is that true, son?" Camden lowered himself to eye level with the boy.

"Yes sir." John was brave and wasn't afraid of facing consequences.

"You know how dangerous that was? What if something happened to you or Carnell's boy?"

"I know, Dad, but I wouldn't have gotten hurt."

"The processing plant is no place for boys to play—understand?" Now go and wash up for dinner before your Ma takes a stick to you. We'll keep this between us this time."

"Is that all you gonna say to the boy?" Kennelly asked. "Seems that things done changed 'round here. If a nigga made my boy do that, well I'd . . ."

"You'd what? They're boys. I don't see the harm in two boys having fun."

"Most decent white folks would've done sumpthin' 'bout that. You should be more careful 'bout what you let your son play with."

"Black doesn't come off. You just tend to the plant's business and leave my son to me."

Kennelly left, mumbling, "Camden's a nigger lover. He went back to his office to phone his wife. When she answered the phone, he told her that Camden was getting' soft on blacks. Miller heard the whole thing and came out from under the desk. "Mister, is John in trouble?

Kennelly rocked back in his swivel chair like a sheriff in a one-horse town. "If he were my son, I'd have killed him."

"I don't wanna get in trouble."

"Then don't play with niggers. Say *nigger*."

"Nigger," Miller repeated.

"You know what a nigger is, don't you?" Miller shook his head no. "That's the proper name for black people. You understand?"

Miller said, "Un-huh. Mathew, too?"

"All of them, Miller. And, don't call him Mathew; that's a good Christian name, too good for him. Call them all niggers. That's what they are."

Adelaide walked through the processing' plant entry into the offices just in time to hear the last part of Kennelly's advice to her son. She smiled in agreement. I didn't expect more from her. After all she was a daughter of the State of Mississippi.

Back in the grove, John couldn't leave well enough alone. He had to one-up Mathew. He convinced Mathew to go back in the processin' plant and the two of them scaled the ladder leadin' to the thin, metal pipe overhead.

They made it half way across. Mathew led; John followed close behind. Kennelly had been waitin' for a second chance to scare the crap out of the boys. He stayed hidden until the boys climbed up to the pipes parallel to the ceilin'.

The boys were concentratin' on crossin' over to the other side. They didn't notice Kennelly holdin' onto the expansion valve which controlled the steam press. When he opened the valve, the pipe immediately got too hot for the boys to maintain their grips. They fell with a *thud* like two shot birds.

The side of the vat broke John's fall. He struck his head as he fell, but still managed to land without breakin' any bones. Mathew fell into the vat and landed on top of a rusty pipe. It ripped through his liver. He was bleedin', bleedin' heavy.

Kennelly called Camden from the office. John was unconscious when his father got to him. Camden managed to wake John for a few minutes at a time. John's first question was, "Is Mathew all right?"

"Kennelly, where is Mathew?" Camden asked.

"He's inside the vat. He's probably bleeding into the juice. Now we aint' gonna be able to sell that juice to anybody. Goddamn waste. Hope that little bastard drowns in there. I told you about that boy. He's costing us money."

"Costing me money. You don't own anything around here!" Camden pointed. "Get him out of there!"

Kennelly stood still, unmoved by the order. "I don't want a nigger bleeding on me."

"Get him out of there or find another job."

Kennelly climbed the ladder and then lowered himself to the top of the press. He tossed Mathew over the side like a sack of potatoes. Camden pulled him down.

"That nigger ain't gonna make it," said Kennelly. I told him about climbing up there like an ape."

John slipped in and out of consciousness.

"We got to get these boys to the hospital. Closest hospital is Colored Hospital. That's about ten miles south. Whitestone Memorial is twenty-two miles north. Did anybody send for Carnell?" Camden asked.

I arrived on my buckboard and looked at Mathew. It was serious. "I need some bindin'. "Gotta stop some of the bleedin' now or this boy's gonna die.

"What happened, son?" I asked John.

"The pipe got hot. Couldn't hold on. Mathew fell in." John closed his eyes slowly.

"Get some ice and some salt Camden. He'll be all right. Just hurry." I wrapped John's head with the salt and ice to reduce the swellin'. "Son, you're gonna have a hell of a headache, but you'll be fine. Let's get them in the truck; they're going to need a doctor."

Kennelly backed the truck up to the plant door. John was gently lifted to the flatbed. Mathew's blood pumped through the binding and onto the floor. He wasn't moving at all. I tightened the dressing and then stuck a wad of cloth in the hole to slow Mathew's bleedin'. Me and Camden lifted Mathew's broken body to the back of the truck then jumped on ourselves. Kennelly put the engine in gear, drivin' quickly toward the main road.

At the intersection, he made the left northward. I was tendin' to the boys, but I noticed immediately.

"Murphy, Colored Hospital is just ten miles away. Both our sons can get help there. Dr. Shaw will fix your boy right up. Whitestone is more than twenty miles away. You know they won't touch my boy. If we go there, my son will die."

Camden looked toward the road ahead and then down at his semi-conscious son. "My son took a pretty bad fall . . . but he's not bleeding to death . . . but if he does . . . "

"—He won't die. Turn this heap around, Murphy. For God's sake, turn this truck around!"

Camden slapped the back of the cab. "Kennelly, take us to Colored Hospital—do it now!"

"I don't know where it is; I'm not colored."

"Turn around now, Kennelly!" Kennelly slowed down but didn't change directions. "Carnell, can you drive?" Camden asked.

"No, I don't own an automobile."

Kennelly scolded Camden. "Are you going to put a colored in front of your own son? Camden Murphy, those savages put a spell on you. I will NOT put that boy's life in danger for a nigger."

Goddamn shame but I know it's what Camden wanted to hear. He was a father, and his son was going in and out of consciousness. Camden gave in to his own fears and turned to me for my okay. I couldn't give it.

"Murphy, I'll make sure somebody at Whitestone looks after your boy. You have my word. He'll be treated as though he was one of mine." I couldn't believe that Camden would ask me to put my son's life in the hands of known racists, heartless bastards.

"Stop the truck; stop the truck now!" I commanded. "You know as well as I do that you can't keep that promise. I'm not gonna let my boy bleed to death like a run-over dog. He's got a better chance out here." Anger covered my face like a wide-brimmed hat.

The truck came to a screeching halt. I lifted Mathew from the back of the truck and laid him in the tall grass in a cool spot. Camden looked tortured as the truck rolled back onto the highway toward Whitestone. I wish I had a shotgun because I would have killed them both and drove the boys to the hospital right before they locked me up.

The road was a busy one. Car after car motored past. I tried to flag each one down, telling the story as quickly as I could to the passing motorists. "My boy is dying; he needs help, please,

please. It took nearly an hour before someone stopped.

"Lady, please, he's a boy. If you believe in God . . . if you believe in Jesus . . .if you believe in anything . . ."

The white woman hesitated then drove ahead. She went nearly a thousand feet before backing up. "Where are you taking him?" she asked me.

"Colored Hospital. God bless you; God bless you."

I loaded Mathew's limp body into the car, apologizing for the blood. We arrived at Colored Hospital in no time. Mathew's liver was finished. Doc Shaw said that hope was in short supply, but he'd had some success swapping livers in raccoons.

At Whitestone, John lapsed in and out of a coma over the next three days, but your mother was able to talk to him enough to get the whole story before he went unconscious for the last time. The pressure of blood inside his skull was crushing his brain. He woke up and asked his father for two people: his mother; and your brother, Mathew. Adelaide, Terri, and Miller were present, but Mathew was at Colored Hospital receiving treatment.

"Daddy, its not Mathew's fault," John said over and over again. He was tired and in a lot of pain, but he kept repeatin' it again and again.

"Mat didn't want to do it. I made him do it. Kennelly, he's mean. He made the pipes hot."

Doctors at Whitestone told Camden and Adelaide that John would die within a few days unless the pressure in his skull relieved itself. It didn't. John's body was on life support, but his spirit was already gone.

Your Momma heard about John's sure death and asked Adelaide to meet in the grove to talk about their sons. Adelaide agreed to the meetin', but she didn't want to.

Your Momma said to Adelaide, "Your son is gone now, but my son lives. Mathew needs a liver and your son doesn't have use for his anymore. You're a mother. You know how precious children are. My son needs a chance. You can give him one," Momma said.

"I can't do that. John is white; Mathew is colored. They just can't swap parts like that."

"Wait, Adelaide, the doctor told us that it might work. He's done this type of surgery before. We just need a liver to try.

"I'd like to help you, but it just wouldn't be right to put a white liver in a brown body. The whole town would be talkin' about it. It's hard enough as it is. Besides, don't they have to be from the same family or something like that? It would never work. Those boys are as different as night and day. I couldn't handle them cutting up my son to get his liver out. I don't want my boy to have those ugly scars when he meets Jesus in heaven."

"Adelaide, just let us try. Nobody has to know where the liver came from—please, I'm begging you."

"I'll talk to Camden, but I can't make no promises."

"That's all I'm asking," Momma said hopefully.

****

Pop stopped talking and walked into the woods after telling me the story. There had to be more, but he wasn't ready to talk about all of it yet. I respected the pain he endured to re-live those memories, but I had to know the rest. I didn't see any connection between Mathew's death, Miller's drowning, and Pop's story. My head was spinning. I took a few spoons of Dr. John's Tonic. Minutes later, I was feeling no pain.

Chapter 13

Friday morning the pickers descended on the house for their wages. They gathered into a small group before the sun climbed high in the sky. Pop wasn't awake early. I suspected he came home late from the lake.

I offered them coffee but they refused it. The workers stood with outstretched hands. "Please pay," the spokesman said. I didn't need any Spanish to understand what they were asking for.

I didn't see Pop walk up behind me. He took quiet steps when he wanted to. "Pay them," he said. I turned around to face him before answering. "Pay them what you owe them," he said again.

"With what?" I asked.

"Money," Pop said.

"How much do I pay them?" I reached into my pocket and pulled out about 1200 dollars. "Will this be enough to cover payroll?"

"Depends on how much you owe 'em."

Pop was being sarcastic. I didn't like it, and I think the workers got irritated, too. He finally stepped forward.

"*Papel,*" said Pop. Each one of the workers pulled out a piece of paper with numbers and initials next to it. He collected the papers and went inside, but not before saying a polite "*Momentito, por favor.*"

Pop came out of the house with a stack of cash and a ledger. He pulled a chair from inside of the house and sat it at the top of the stairs. One by one he called out names. "Carballo, Nieves, Sandoval." When all the names were finished he picked up the chair and went back into the house. I looked back and the crowd was already gone.

"If you're running a business, the first thing you better know is how everybody gets paid," he said.

"I'm not running a business, you are. I was just trying to help out."

"Just goes to show that you got no future in the orange business. Stick to what you know. Why don't you go home, son."

"Are we on that again?"

"We're gonna be on that 'til you leave. This is no place for a doctor."

"I haven't been a doctor since I arrived."

"Then what are you, boy?"

"I am a son—son of a—."

"If you say it, you're gonna get the backside of my hand," Pop promised.

"Say what? I was going to say son of a stubborn old mule who happens to be one of the smartest businessmen I've ever known.

"You were gonna say all that?" he asked with a subtle smile. "What you want for breakfast, then. I'll make you the works. Fish and grits."

"That's fine, Pop, but I only said it 'cause I meant it."

"I didn't call you a liar. I just like the way you say smartest businessman. I think that's worth fryin' a little snook and makin' a hot pot of cheese grits.

"You must be awfully smart to make Camden pay you what he does."

"Got nothin' to do with smart. He's payin' what he owes, not a penny more."

"What he owes? You said you make as much money as me. It doesn't add up. I don't care how many oranges those Mexicans pick out there, I can't get to $140,000."

"You want gravy?"

"No, Pop, but I'll take a few grand if you got it lying around."

"What's that suppose to mean?"

"You had a lot of cash in the house. Knowing the way you are, that wasn't the last of the money."

"Mexicans don't cash checks. You see a bank around here? Besides, Camden ain't the only one payin' me."

"Since I've been home, Murphy's Grove is the only place you've taken me. Who else are you supplying labor to?"

"Murphy is not my only customer. You like your grits stiff or runny?

"*Stiff*—Is that all you're going to say about it?"

"What else needs to be said? I do all right," he said while he continued to do payroll.

The sound of a truck pulling up outside stopped the conversation. Kennelly got out of the truck with something in his hand.

"I told that old bastard never to set foot on my property. He's gonna die today."

Pop shut off the stove and hustled out the back door. I went through the front door to meet Kennelly.

"Can I help you?" I asked, nervously looking back over my shoulder to see if Pop was behind me.

"Yup." Kennelly handed me an envelope.

"What's this?" I asked as I looked at the naked white envelope. The workers pulled away quickly then quickly disappeared. I have no idea where they went, but not one stayed for the fireworks.

"If it ain't got your name on it, then it probably ain't for you," he said disrespectfully.

"It doesn't have anybody's name on it. So what's in it?"

"Listen, boy, I was told to drop this off. That's what I'm doin'. Don't get cheeky with me. I don't have to answer to a colored—got it?" Like a bully, Kennelly stabbed me in the chest with his index finger.

"Move out the way, son. I believe this man is trespassin' on private property." Pop had a bead on Kennelly. The hammer was already cocked.

"C'mon Pop, put that away before somebody gets hurt."

"Nigger, you don't have the guts!"

Bang! Pop shot Kennelly in the leg.

"*Ooh damn*, you *really* shot him!"

"He's trespassin' ain't he? I told him never to come on my property as long as I live. I got a sign out there. It's been there since your Momma died. This is the second time in a week. I thought I'd give him somethin' to think about."

"You half-breed bastard!" Kennelly yelled. He was staring incredulously at the hole torn into his pants by Pop's bullet.

"I'm gonna count to three . . . it would be wise to remove yourself from my land. One, two . . ." Pop counted.

"Stop! You just can't go around shooting people," I hollered.

"This here, boy, is Ocala, not Fort Lauderdale. A man gets a fair warnin' to get off another man's property. If he don't move, then he gets what he deserves."

Bang!

"You shot him again. Have you lost your mind?"

"Yeah, I did. The next one is gonna be a headshot. Kennelly, I'm countin' again. This time I'm gonna give you to five. One, two, three . . ."

Bang!

"Oops, 'half-breed bastards' can't count that high," Pop said.

Kennelly lay on the dirt, shot in a major vessel in his leg. Blood was pumping out through his fingers. I couldn't leave him because Pop would surely have killed him.

"Give me the gun. Now, Pop, give me the damn gun!"

"Okay, son. Clean him up and get his ass off my land."

I thought it was over but it wasn't. Pop had more for him.

"Hey, Kennelly, I thought you Irishmen bleed green. *Bang*. Seems like that luck-of-the-Irish thing was a lie too."

Pop surrendered the gun to me without any real resistance. He sat on the front porch and watched as Kennelly's life force leaked from four holes in his legs. I ran into the house to get a few rags and some alcohol.

"Give him some tonic, son; it'll help him with the pain."

I tore the rags into tourniquets, all the while in disbelief that my father had really shot Kennelly, a white man, a white man in Ocala. *Dammit*.

Pop teased from the porch. "Hey, Kennelly, my son is a doctor. He could save your life, but I'm sure you don't want a colored touchin' you." He was like Julius Caesar watching the Christian gladiators being torn to pieces by the lion. It was sport.

"Son, he's gonna need a doctor. Nearest hospital is Charles Drew Hospital. It used to be called Colored Hospital. It's about ten miles south of here. Ain't that right, Kennelly? Or would you like to go to Whitestone?"

"Pop, call an ambulance. He's going into shock."

"Son, they'll never get here in time. That cracker's gonna die. The best thing is to drive him to the hospital. I'll help you put him on the truck.

Pop came off the porch. He walked around to the back of the house. He took a pretty long time. A distance away, I heard the sound of a motor starting. It made a lot of noise and I smelled burning oil. It was the old flatbed truck Pop used to drive after Mathew died. He backed it up to Kennelly.

"One, two, three lift."

Kennelly was on the back of rust bucket. I jumped up there with Kennelly for the ride to the hospital. Pop threw the truck in gear. At the intersection, we turned south to Charles Drew. The truck was doing a furious 12 miles per hour. Kennelly was frightened, but stubbornly defiant.

"Where are we?" Kennelly asked through the delirium of pain. "We're goin' south, aren't we boy?"

"Yes, we're headed for Charles Drew Hospital. We'll be there in a couple of minutes."

"Don't take me to Colored Hospital. I'll die there. Whitestone. Take me to Whitestone."

"The man said Whitestone—didn't he, son?"

Pop waited until he was practically at the doorstep of Colored Hospital before turning around to go north toward Whitestone. He jerked a u-turn and slowed even more.

"Hey, Kennelly, where exactly is Whitestone Memorial? I ain't no cracker; I don't know where it is," Pop said. He lied.

By the time we got to Whitestone Memorial, Kennelly's legs were the color of four-day-old ground beef at room temperature. He'd lost a great deal of blood and complaining that he couldn't feel his legs. We later found out that a white-hot slug spinning through flesh and bone had severed his spinal cord.

Later that day Pop and I were talking on the porch. "Pop, did you hear? Kennelly is going to be paralyzed from the waist down."

"I wasn't aimin' for his spine. I was tryin' to shoot him in the ding-a-ling. Guess I'm a bad shot, huh?

"What are we going to do when the police show up for you?" I asked, referring to the consequences of shooting a white man in Ocala.

"What you worryin' about that for son. You oughtta be celebratin' boy; you're a hero! You saved that man's life." Pop's mood turned mildly serious. "There's gonna be an investigation. We need to mark the spot where Kennelly bled on my property."

Pop was amused by the whole thing and pretty certain that he'd beat any charges filed against him.

"Son, he's gonna make it, right?"

"Yes, he'll make it."

"How long do you think it will take him to figure out he's lost a part of himself?"

"Not long."

"Good," he said, "Now he'll know how I feel. I don't want him to die; I want him to live so he can get what he was supposed to get a long time ago. He killed your brother. Camden knows it, and I know it. Both those boys had burned hands. The only way that pipe could have gotten hot was if somebody opened the pressure release valve. He and Camden were the only two who could have done it. Camden would have never hurt his own son."

Pop was gloating.

"Why don't you spend some time with Camden's daughter tonight, just to celebrate? You said that y'all was just talkin'."

"That's sick, Pop."

"One down," he said, "one to go."

Chapter 14

The police finally showed up at the house, sirens blaring and lights on. They pulled right up to the front door and came out of the car with guns drawn.

"Carnell Murphy, come out with your hands up!"

I yelled through the window, "We're coming out. Don't shoot."

"Toss out your weapons. Do it now!" the policeman shouted.

"The gun is under the pail near the back porch. There are no other weapons," I said.

Pop and I walked out slowly with our hands up. One of the officers slammed me to the ground. The other officer kept his gun pointed at Pop while a third officer cuffed us both.

"What happened here, Carnell?"

"Hi'ya, Jim. Got some of that orange barbecue sauce in a bottle. Make sure you get it before you leave," Pop said, as though he were in the church parking lot after Bible study.

"I'll get it, Carnell. Now tell me why you had to go and shoot Kennelly?"

"Trespassin', Jim. I was under the law. Go over there an' look. He bled on my property." Pop pointed toward the dirt road.

"You just can't go around shootin' people. That ain't neighborly."

"Didn't you pass that sign out there?"

"What sign, Carnell?"

Pop pointed. "The no trespassin' sign that's cemented in the ground next to the mailbox."

"Yeah, I see it," Jim said shaking his head over the whole event.

"A reasonable man would respect that, Jim."

"You got a permit for that gun?"

"Sure do?"

"Where is it? I need to see it."

"Want me to get it, Jim?"

"Yeah, I'll walk you in." The three of us walked casually toward the front door. "Is your boy visitin' from outta town?"

"Mm-hmm. I'm tryin' to make him go home. He's been here too long already. Don't want him to get in any trouble."

"Okay, where is it, Carnell."

Pop pointed to his bedroom wall. On the wall were pieces of the United States Constitution.

"Jim, see right there where it gives me the right to bear arms and defend myself. That's my permit, all the permit I need. The man was trespassin', Jim."

Jim ushered the two of us toward the front door. "I'm still gonna have to take you in until we get this sorted out. How long you an' Kennelly's been goin' at it? More than thirty years, I bet."

"'Bout that. I've never trespassed on his property. What makes him think he can come to mine?"

"Y'all been feudin' since I was ten. You are too damn old to keep this up, Carnell."

"I gave him a chance, didn't I son? I counted several times for him to leave the way he came. I was 'fraid he might do somethin' to me and my son. Jim, this the second time he did this in a week. I can't have him disrespectin' my home, can I? Let me show you somethin'."

Pop walked Jim around to the side of the house where he pointed to the ground.

"Dig right there."

"For what?"

"The warnin' shots I gave the first time he came here with Terri Murphy, Camden's daughter."

Jim kneeled and pulled his keychain utility knife from his uniform pocket. He dug in the holes and pulled out two smattered pieces of metal.

"See, I told you. If you don't believe me call Terri. She'll tell you."

"All right, all right. Turn 'im loose." The assistant deputy unlocked the handcuffs while Jim looked around some more. Carnell, don't leave town. You might still have some splainin' to do."

"Now where is an old man like me goin'? I got to run my business."

"You may have to stay awhile longer than you planned," Officer Jim said to me. "I may need to get a statement from you."

"Are there going to be charges filed?" I asked.

"Don't know yet, but I gotta take your Daddy's gun. That crazy old coot is right about trespassin'. If his story checks out, there ain't nothin' we can do."

"Really?"

"That don't mean that he's out of the woods. Kennelly may sue him under civil law. That's his right."

"Jim? Would you mind givin' my son a ride to the bus station? He's goin' home today."

"I don't need a ride. Didn't you hear the man say not to leave town?"

"I heard him, but his investigation will be over in a few minutes. Here comes Camden's girl."

Terri's approach was fast and hard. The car tires kicked up a small cloud of orange dust. She slammed on the brakes of the car and jumped out. The car was still rolling when her foot hit the ground.

"What in the hell is goin' on? Kennelly's wife called and said that he had been shot over here. What in the name of Jesus happened?"

Pop walked through the house and onto the back porch. He yelled out to Officer Jim, "Don't forget your orange barbecue sauce," leaving me to answer Terri's questions.

"Kennelly was trespassing. Pop shot him after a warning."

"Trespassing? He was bringing a check from my father to pay for the work already done. I had to go to Tampa early this morning or I would have brought it myself."

"Have you ever brought a check here before? My father says you have never been on the property until you came to complain about the pickers."

"Your Daddy has never been this sick. He normally gets his check at the grove or your cousin Margaret picks it up."

"Everybody knows that Pop and Kennelly are enemies. That wasn't smart at all. The last time you two came here, Pop fired two warning shots into the ground."

"I heard it but I didn't know that's what it was. I thought he was just cleaning his gun. That happens all the time around here. By the way, I didn't send Kennelly over here."

"Well, if you didn't send him, who did?"

Terri paused before answering. "Daddy is the only person other than me authorized to write a check, but Daddy wouldn't have sent him either."

"—Are you sure about that, Terri?"

"I'm headed home right now to find out. I'll call you. What's your phone number? Never mind, I have it at the house."

Officer Jim approached Terri. "Ms. Murphy, did Carnell warn Kennelly to stay off his property the other day?"

"Well, yes, but . . ."

"—Thank you, that's all I need. Give Carnell back his gun," Jim said to the other officer. "Terri, you may need to make yourself available just in case the State Attorney needs you." Jim moved a little closer and whispered to Terri, "When you gonna let me take you out again for some more pickup truck love?"

"You can pick me up tonight at around eight."

"You mean it?"

"Hell no!" Terri jumped into her car and sped back toward Murphy's Grove.

Later that evening after the cops had gone, the phone rang. It was Terri.

"What took you so long?" I asked

"You ever tried talking to a rock? I couldn't get anything out of my father except 'Kennelly should have left when Carnell told him to.'"

"What happens now? Who's going to manage the processing plant?"

"Me," she said. "Those machines practically run themselves."

"You? No offense, but suppose they get stuck or break? I bet you're going to tell me that you can handle a wrench."

"I can. Remember, my father doesn't have any sons left. After Momma died, there was nobody to tell Daddy what I shouldn't learn. I am a quick study. Anyway, I'd like to get together to finish our talk," she said.

"Pick up where we left off?" I asked

"Uh-huh. You don't have any problems with that, do you?"

"None whatsoever. I just have to make sure that my father has what he needs. Two spoons of Doc John's and he'll be fine. How's Camden's supply holding up?"

"Not too good. Daddy's almost finished with the bottle. It seems that he's drinking that stuff much faster these days. How about Carnell?"

"Last I checked he had a full bottle left. I looked at my watch then I looked at Terri. "So what time and where do you want to meet?"

"The same place, same time. It'll give me some time to finish up some paperwork. On second thoughts, let's drive to the river," said Terri. "We can meet at the lake and then take one car."

"Is that safe?" I asked

"Safe how?"

"For us to be driving in the same car at night? I don't want any trouble."

"You mean the Midnight Riders?" she asked.

"Whatever you want to call them."

"I wouldn't worry about it Kenneth. They aren't that active here. Ocala is theirs already. You've probably got more activity in Fort Lauderdale than we have here. They've quietly spread to other places."

"So, they don't have a camp near the river—do they?"

"The closest place that they have is a camp about twenty to twenty-five miles outside of town. They're further out than Whitestone Hospital. Like I said, Kenneth Luke, you don't have to worry about them."

"Terri, maybe we ought to hang around here. I think our fathers are going to need us nearby. "

"You're not scared, are you?" Terri asked. "If you are, I understand. You've been away for a long time. Fort Lauderdale is a long way from Ocala. I suppose you've come to rely on other people to protect you.

"I SAID I'm not scared. I just don't want to stir the pot. People are going to be upset enough about a black shooting a white. "

"*Black?*" Terri asked. "Changed again, huh?"

"Okay, Colored."

"What Color? Never mind. You'll explain later," she said after a short pause.

I didn't know if I could explain. "Only if you insist," I said. "See you then."

Chapter 15

Terri and I met at the lake as planned. She offered to drive as a courtesy and convenience. She said she knew the way to the river and it was easier for her to drive than to give me directions. I thought that there might be another reason.

We were cordial as we drove the twenty-eight miles to the river. It seems that each of us was waiting for the other to break the ice. Tension made the 28 miles feel like 80. Whether eight miles or eight inches, it was a long distance to travel if I needed help. I couldn't put my fingers on it but something was wrong, I felt it in my bones.

The underbrush around the river was alive. As we made our way to the shoreline, we heard animals, flying, running and jumping out of the truck's path and away from the prying white light thrown from the headlamps.

"You want to get out?" Terri asked.

After a thought, I said, "In a minute." I was stalling. I didn't want to leave the safety of the truck. Each new sound made me nauseous.

"We'd come out here a lot when I was young," Terri said. "We'd wade across the shallows looking for salamanders and small fish. This river used to be lined with people. It was a good place to fish, but my family didn't do much fishing on family outings. They preferred to hunt wild rabbit."

"What kind of rabbit?" I asked, like I cared.

"They caught a lot of black rabbits."

"I'd bet those rabbits didn't have a chance."

"They'd set traps near the water where there were footprints. Usually, it didn't take more than an hour or two to catch at least one."

"Did you eat what you caught?" I asked.

"Mom did. Daddy and I wouldn't eat much rabbit. We weren't much on hunting. Daddy said there was no challenge. Momma didn't care about challenge; she just loved fresh meat. She'd tear the flesh off the bones. I'd cry if I saw them alive, but Momma would say God gave us dominion over those poor, stupid creatures. She'd say that a rabbit's place in the world was to provide food for the stronger animals including us."

"Did you buy it, Terri?"

"Not really, but you want to believe everything your Momma tells you—I know I did."

"I understand that."

"Miller was like Momma; John was gentle like Daddy. Miller loved black rabbit. He'd see one and chase it for hours. I remember he caught one by the legs and flung it into the tree. It was odd to see a four-year-old boy do that. John was just the opposite. He hated the rabbit hunts."

"Did John ever tell you why?"

"I heard him talking to one of the boys about how he didn't see the fun in fighting with something that won't fight back."

"John was right."

"Yes, that was John."

"What about you? What kind of person are you?" I asked.

"I guess I'm in the middle, sometimes sensitive, other times hard. I do what I have to do. Is that a problem?" Terri asked.

"Hey, don't get defensive. I was just asking a question."

We both paused to gather our thoughts. I restarted the conversation.

"I've been gone a long time, Terri. What's happened to Ocala?" I was talking like I had an understanding of the entire city. I did not. What I knew of Ocala was everything inside the fence surrounding the grove, and even there, I wasn't sure.

"Time happened, "Terri said. "As a doctor, I'd expect you to know a lot about that. You don't expect anything to stay the same—do you?

"No, but this type of change seems forced. It doesn't seem like natural evolution to me. Wouldn't you expect our fathers to be the best of friends after nearly forty years?"

Terri paused. "I guess, but old habits die hard, especially with old timers like them."

"Mr. Clark hasn't changed much," I said. "But, you made him smile, and he called me by my name. That's progress to me."

"Could it be that you've changed? That those things were going on all along but you were too scared or too young to notice?"

"I guess that would be a fair assessment." A thought popped into my head. "Terri, would you mind if I asked you how Ms. Adelaide died?" The question caught her off guard.

". . .Cancer, and a broken heart."

"And Ms. Elizabeth?" she asked.

"A broken heart." I paused and added, "But high blood pressure got the blame."

"What about Mathew? What were you told about your brother's death?" Terri asked.

"Where did that come from? We were talking about mothers."

"Stop stalling and answer the question," she pushed

"Best I can tell, he fell into the orange press and damaged his liver. He needed a transplant, but we couldn't find a donor."

"That's not the story I was told."

"What were you told, Terri?"

"I heard Mathew died from the fall. He was dead on arrival to the hospital."

"Who told you that?"

"My Momma."

"That's what she wanted you to believe. My brother died because we couldn't get him a liver transplant in time to save his life."

Terri spoke slowly, "What about John's liver, why didn't they use his?"

I gave Terri time to think about what she'd asked before answering her question. "They needed parental consent to harvest John's liver."

"Oh."

"John was dead. He didn't need it," I said.

"Maybe my parents didn't know that this could be done."

"Do you really believe that, Terri?"

"No," she said apologetically, "I don't."

Two people had an epiphany at once. In deference to our families, neither one of us would say what we knew. We just silently started the healing process, two people at a time.

After our non-verbal confession, I asked Terri if it be all right if we left the river. She wasn't ready to go and preferred to lose herself in my arms. Terri scooped up my hand and placed it in her lap. She squeezed it gently, but held on. The prism through which she viewed past events was cracked and flawed, but she didn't realize it until our conversation at the river.

We shared why we left and why we came back. We spoke of our fathers and familial duty. We spoke of opportunities lost and loves past. When we were finished, she and I were spent. We embraced as if we'd made love for hours on end. Perspiration rolled down the valley of each of our backs. Terri's face was buried in my shoulders and facing north. My neck was straight as I peered through the black film into the starry southern sky.

Click! Thoom!

The passenger door cracked open with no warning and little time for response. A strong hand yanked me from Terri's arms to the damp carpet of leaves and mud. My feet flailed behind me as I was dragged quickly through the woods. "Drive away now, nigger-lovin' whore." These words were the last I heard before the slamming of the door and the turning of the van's engine.

The woods opened to a dirt clearing. The charred cross was smoldering and I heard chants of Heil! Heil! Heil! The ox dragging me let me go and

I rose to my feet, bleeding but feeling no pain, thanks to the adrenaline pumping feverishly through my bruised body.

The circle closed around me.

“Nigger, nigger, nigger . . .”

I dusted myself off and held my head up like an African chieftain.

“Nigger, nigger, nigger . . .”

“Who are you? I asked, vaguely recognizing some of the faces from town, maybe the hospital, or possibly childhood. Why are you doing this to me?”

“Nigger, nigger, nigger . . .”

The circle closed tighter. Hands went up in the Nazi salute. “White power!” they boomed.

I stood quietly and waited for compassion and sensibility to descend on the throng of angry white faces.

“Guilty, guilty, guilty . . .”

“I’ve done nothing wrong. I’m a doctor.”

A lone figure emerged from the crowd. His intensity was insincere—passionless. His words came from a dark place, but they were not his. The ugliness spewing from his mouth was taught to him during his indoctrination. I could sense that, if not for the press of the crowd, he’d turn and run. He had not tasted blood yet. I was to be his first kill. This was his initiation.

"Our brother was shot by this coon's father. Eye for an eye, brothers!" he roared."

I recognized the main instigator. He was the young man wearing the Black Sabbath T-shirt in the hospital cafeteria. "I know you," I said. "You work at Whitestone Memorial."

His eyes glistened as he marshaled his courage to strike. Out in the brush, he had to prove himself a man, instead of a pimple-faced teenager making minimum wage to swing a mop.

"He wants to know what he's done, brothers. Should we tell him?"

The group chanted the same refrain, "Tell him, tell him, tell him . . ."

He moved closer to me. His crystal blue eyes betrayed him. He was weak and as scared as I. He stopped two inches from my face and shouted.

"You're a god-damn, nigger, that's what you've done!" His voice was steely, empty. He burned away his fear in the intensity of the senseless berserker rage. "Eye for an eye, brothers!" The others responded to the call. "Eye for an eye!"

Whump!

He punched me to the ground. The mob descended on me with a flurry of kicks, chops, and elbows. I was pounded into muddy red clay. My body stripped the skin from their knuckles. I drifted in and out of consciousness. The pain dulled as the assault continued.

"Can you swim, nigger? I said, CAN YOU SWIM?"

Two of the gang stepped forward to hold my arms out while a third practiced his swing with a Louisville Slugger. He broke an arm and leg. I heard the bones snap. They dragged me to the rivers edge and rolled me in. A foot shoved me away from shore and into the deep.

I opened my mouth to breathe and the river water rushed in, drowning my words and with it, any chance to call for help. I drifted downward toward the bottom and then back up near the surface. I was less than two inches from the surface but hadn't the strength to reach it.

Before blacking out I heard gunfire. That's all I remembered, that and the feeling of angels lifting me from the water into the air. I must have been hallucinating.

I regained consciousness for a moment. A moment was long enough to feel pain, pain so intense it hurt at the cellular level. I was alone and bleeding in the woods. Death was coming too slowly. I called to it, but it didn't come. It couldn't hear me through the chunks of meat and body fluids filling my mouth. I gurgled, but no words broke free of my swollen lips.

My kick-blurred vision cleared enough to see shapes and forms. Someone was moving toward me. I balled my fist and waited like a trap door spider. A foot shoved me over, but still I waited. The figure bent down to get a closer look and I swung with all my might to bring it down. I passed out before I could see who was on the end of my punch. Pop said there'd be consequences—and, he was right.

Chapter 16

Healer, heal thyself. My skin hurt, my toenails hurt, my hair hurt. I couldn't find one safe place to touch that didn't send me writhing in pain. The nurse came in to change my head dressing. She had to look away to keep from running out of the room. Just the way she asked "Who did this to you?" gutted me like a catfish.

"Nurse, where am I?" I asked through swollen gums and loose teeth. The words scratched my throat before escaping through the half-inch split in my bruised lips. My breath stank of dried blood. The huge lump on my head was soft to the touch and contained most of my short-term memory. I had no idea how long I'd been out of it.

It was surreal—the river—the shots—the young janitor. I couldn't believe that it happened. I dragged my hand from my side to feel for the bruises, cuts, and gashes. My fingers slowly crawled down my leg. One by one, they fell into punch-outs of skin, fat, and meat caused by the strike of cowboy boots against soft tissue over bone. My skin was stitched together like two thick scraps of leather. The lines zigzagged in several directions. The stitches felt like zippers. Each inch of movement made me want to holler.

I turned my head to the side to see if anyone else was in my room. Bubbling red saliva dribbled from my mouth like a chipped cup. Company would have been good—just someone to lament to—a place to empty my embarrassment and pain, but I was alone. I wondered if Pop knew what happened to me. He couldn't know. If he knew, he would have been at the hospital, ready to take me out, away from Whitestone and white people.

The phone was arm's length away. I reached over and pulled it from the white pine nightstand and onto the bed. I lifted the handset from the base and started to dial. Each pressed digit made me curse the joints, sinew, and muscles of my hand. After a brief pause, the number rang through. The answer came on the fourth ring. "Hello," the voice answered exuberantly, "this is Dr. Kenneth L. Murphy. I'm unavailable at the moment, but please leave a message." I'd gotten in the habit of leaving some inspirational quote at the end of the message. I listened for it. "As Dr. King said, 'If you haven't found something to die for, you aren't worthy to live.' *Beeeep*." Ironically, I was trying to call my father when I dialed my own home. I tried to remember my father's phone number but couldn't.

I reclined in bed trying to piece together the events that put me in the hospital. I had been beaten; that was clear from the bruises. The fact that several shots had been fired was not in dispute. I remember being at the river, but not much more. Terri. She was with me when I got yanked from the van. I couldn't remember who found me or how I arrived at the hospital. The devil was in the details that I couldn't recall.

The nurse walked in to adjust my intravenous fluids and check wound drainage. She didn't speak. She just went about the business of measuring, collecting, and recording information. My eyelids were swollen. Perhaps she couldn't tell if I was sleeping or not. She deserved the benefit of the doubt.

"Nurse," I moaned. "Do you know how I got here?" She flipped to the front of my chart and read, never making eye contact with me. She found what she was looking for and hung my patient records from a holder at the foot of my bed.

"A good Samaritan," she answered as though giving me the time.

"Does it say who?"

"Does it matter? You should be grateful you're alive."

"Yes, I am grateful—to the person who found me and the people who helped me. I owe you all, *Nurse Conway*? I'd like to be able to thank him like I'm thanking you now."

She was slow to tell, but after she returned from emptying my Foley bag she said, "His name is Camden Murphy. It's a good thing he was out there. You didn't have much time. What were you doing out at the river at that time anyway?"

"Ocala baptism." Nurse Conway understood what I meant even though I didn't give the answer much thought. Purification was, perhaps, a better answer. My thoughts were interrupted by a lone figure standing in the doorway. I rocked myself forward to get a better look at my visitor. It was Camden.

I gestured for him to enter. He waddled in looking a little more than tired. I waved again to draw him closer. He stepped forward to the bed rail and held on with his strong side. "Please sit, I said."

I waited for him to say something about my appearance, but he didn't. I surmised that I looked worse when he fished me out of the mud, but I couldn't be sure. Like my father, Camden was a man of few words. Out of respect for the silence and the man, I waited for him to speak first.

"I'm not going to ask you how you're feeling; I already know. When are you getting out?"

"Don't know. Camden, thank you for helping me."

"You ought to go home when you get out of here. This place is no place for you." Camden pulled out his bottle of Dr. John's Tonic and took a swig.

"Right now, I just want to concentrate on healing," I said.

"I think we all do." Camden's words were bloated like a fat piñata. He sounded just like Pop. Two men, supposedly on opposite ends of the spectrum, more similar than anyone would ever know. If I closed my eyes and listened carefully, the message and the messenger were the same.

"Healing? There are different kinds of healing, Camden. Which one are you talking about?"

Camden held his cane with two hands like Moses in the *Ten Commandments*. I waited to see if he'd do the scene where Moses tells Ramses that the next plague on Egypt would be by his hands. He didn't.

"We're all sick in this town. Some of us have broken hearts and others have broken bodies. Take your pick," he said with equal parts of sadness and disgust.

"I appreciate your visit, but you could have called. Why did you come?"

"I made a promise," Camden boldly announced, "and a Murphy's word is always good. Good as money in the bank."

"Promised whom?" I asked. Camden dropped his eyes and leaned heavily on his cane to hold himself up. His strength was fading in and out as often as my father's.

"Your daddy," he mumbled as though answering for a failure. It took a few minutes before I realized that he was talking about the promise he'd made to my father when Mathew was being taken to Whitestone Hospital long ago. It was a promise that then he couldn't keep.

"That wasn't your fault, Mr. Murphy. It was just the times. You couldn't control what other people did."

"I could control what I did, though. Son, we should have gone to Colored Hospital. We didn't, and it's my fault. If I had been stronger, maybe there would have been a better ending. I bowed to my own fear."

"Understandable," I said. "Any parent faced with that choice would have made the same decision."

"You don't understand. I wasn't afraid for John; I was afraid for me."

I positioned my head to hear the answer he'd give to the next question I would ask. I had a feeling it was going to be big. "In what way, Camden?"

"I didn't want anyone to think that I was a Negro sympathizer. It could have ruined me and my family's reputation. I was wrong; I know that now. Your father knew that then. I don't blame him for not forgiving me."

"Is that what happened between you and my father?" I understood that his silence meant yes.

"I've been trying to make it up to him ever since," Camden said pensively.

Things started to make sense. Pop was right about how many people contributed to Mathew's death. Before talking to Camden, I believed that my father's rumblings were that of a paranoid man whose experiences with racism cropped up in everything he saw.

"It must have been pretty hard for you being at that river again. This is the second time that river almost drowned the life out of you."

I had no idea what Camden was talking about, but I wanted to hear more. "It's been a long time, but I don't remember almost drowning in the river."

"You were very young. I just want to thank you for finding Miller."

I unlocked every memory I had, but I couldn't remember pulling Miller out of the river or any water, for that matter.

"You're welcome," I said mechanically, as if I deserved thanks.

"You almost drowned pulling him out of the water," Camden said, "but you didn't give up."

"Why, then, was my father accused of hurting your son?"

There was a long pause before he answered. "I don't really know. There was some confusion about where Miller was found. Rumor had it that you and Carnell were seen at the lake, not the river, a little before you found Miller at the river.

"But, it was in the river that they—I mean I—found Miller's body, right?"

"Where else could it be? He was covered up on the bank of the river when his mother and I arrived."

Pop said that Miller drowned at the lake, not the river. How could anybody forget something like that? He was old, but not that old.

"Camden, thank you for coming. I'm tired; I just need to rest now." Camden wasn't gone for two minutes before I picked up the phone and called the operator. "I need the number for Carnell Murphy. What city? Ocala." I dialed the number after 6 p.m.

"Pop? When are you coming? We need to talk." I felt the pain move from the outside to the inside when he said that he wouldn't be making the trip to Whitestone.

Chapter 17

I was confined to the hospital for a few days before being released. Terri called a few times but we didn't talk much until she came to see me. It was the first time that I saw her, since the night at the river.

Terri seemed timid, not the girl who slammed me at Reilly's Pharmacy or the girl who negotiated $200 dollars for a twenty dollar bottle of tonic. Her bravado was stripped from her, seemingly by guilt for taking me to the place that nearly cost me my life. It wasn't her fault, but she, like I, believed that Ocala had changed enough for us to be together without fear or intimidation. We were both wrong.

It was a good morning to talk and be together. The drainage tubes had been removed from my legs and lungs. For the first time since being admitted, I had a good night's sleep. She couldn't tell, though, because my face was still swollen and bruised. She touched each of the stitched zippers on my head and face and then worked her way downward. I didn't feel naked until she began to talk about the night at the river. Afterward, I felt not only naked but also vulnerable. Terri talked as though what happened to me was an accident. When she'd finished making me relive the assault she began talking about her brother Miller like he and I had something in common.

"Miller didn't die in the river, he died in the lake," Terri said. I was more confused than ever. Camden said that Miller drowned in the river. Pop said Miller drowned in the lake. Terri was the second vote for the lake.

"Does it really matter where Miller drowned? The point is that he did drown and he's gone."

"It does if he were murdered," she countered, replacing sadness with anger.

"Who murdered Miller? Who would do such a thing to a child?" I asked, enraged at the thought of some sick bastard hurting a child.

"Your Momma, Kenneth, your Momma killed Miller," Terri said somberly.

"My Momma wouldn't hurt a fly, let alone a little boy. You will NOT disrespect the memory of my mother. Get out. Get the hell out!" I yelled.

"Not before you know the whole story," Terri yelled back. "Just hear me out."

I didn't want to hear anything about my mother. She was perfect—kind and gentle—a mother, wife, and friend.

Terri began. "Miller found his way to the lake." Terri took a deep breath, held it, and then let out a long sigh before continuing. "Your Momma was fishing at the lake to pass time, like she did almost every day."

"Go on," I said.

"Miller knew how to get to the lake from our house because John and Mathew would go there all the time and he'd follow them. When John died, Miller thought that he was still alive and playing at the lake so he went to find him."

"And?"

"He was on the homemade raft that the older boys made to cross the lake. Miller accidentally slipped into the water. He couldn't swim."

"What does any of this have to do with my Momma?" I asked.

"My little brother was drowning. Your Daddy had come home from the grove around lunchtime. When he couldn't find your momma in the house, he came to the lake looking for her. As you know, the lake is less than a five minute walk from your backyard into the woods."

I folded my arms and waited for the conclusion of the fable.

"Kenneth, my brother was drowning and your mother did nothing to save him."

"My mother couldn't swim," I said defensively. "They would have sunk like two stones."

"Carnell could. Your mother wouldn't let him save my brother, a boy, dying a horrible death. He was only four, just a frightened baby. He called out for help. 'Nigga help.' *Gurgle.* 'Help, Nigga.' *Bluuup.* 'Help! nigg-' . . . . He disappeared under the water while your parents looked on and did nothing," Terri said, coldly re-living each detail as if she were there when it happened.

The left side of my lip curled when I asked Terri, "Who told you this crap? Kennelly? That agitating, racist mother—"

"Kennelly didn't have to tell me," she said while slowly rubbing her forehead. "I was there."

My mouth dropped. I couldn't believe what Terri told me, nor did I want to. My parents allowed a boy to drown? No. My spirit screamed.

"Why are you telling me about this now?"

"Because I feel awful. You were not responsible for either of my brothers' deaths. When I saw you go down—it was terrible—I didn't want them to kill you," Terri confessed.

"—What did you say?"

"They were only supposed to hurt you. It got out of hand."

"You set me up? YOU SET ME UP!"

Terri burst into tears. "I'm sooo sorry. I'm sorry," she whimpered as she fell back into the chair to console herself. "I was mad at your parents, not at you, Kenneth. You did nothing wrong. You didn't deserve this. My God, what have I done?"

"Was your father in on this?"

"No, oh no. Daddy knew nothing about this."

"Then, how is it that he brought me to this hospital?"

"Daddy brought you here? Oh, Jesus, I didn't know."

"Get out. I need to think." I fought to keep in my emotions, but my eye began to quiver from betrayal and disappointment, anger and pain. "You wicked little tramp" leaped off my tongue on its own.

"I'm sorry," she said again as she picked up her purse and headed quickly for the door.

I lifted the transmitter again and dialed Pop's number. He answered. "Daddy, I get out of the hospital tomorrow. Can you meet me at the bus station with my bag? I just want to go home, back to Fort Lauderdale. I don't belong here. You're right; Ocala is not for me."

The doctor signed my discharge papers at 2 p.m. the next day. I called a cab to take me to the bus station. Pop was already waiting when I pulled up. I pushed my aluminum crutches out of the taxi, one at a time, before struggling to my feet.

I hobbled into the depot and purchased my ticket home. The bus was leaving at 4:30 p.m. I had two and a half hours to kill. I bought a week-old *Newsweek* and found a seat in the small terminal to rest. My father sat beside me.

"What time does your bus leave?" he asked.

"4:30"

"That's a lot of time to wait. If you want, I'll wait with you."

"No, I'll be all right. I'm sure you've got lots of important things to do," I said.

"Not really. I pretty much took care of everything already."

"Go on home, Pop."

"Is that a request or a command?"

"Take it anyway you want. Right now, I don't give a damn."

"You sassin' me, boy?"

"*Man*. I don't appreciate being called boy."

"So you're a man now. When did that happen'?

"Three days ago when I was lying in bed suffering from a severe ass-whooping and my father wouldn't come to see me."

"I warned you, Kenneth. You wouldn't listen."

"That's right Pop, and I paid the price all by myself. I paid in full." I finished his thought for him.

"The important thing, son, is that you're goin' home. That's the best place for you."

I turned to the first feature article in the magazine and began to read, ignoring my father's comments. He began fidgeting in his seat and tapping the armrest on his side.

"So I guess you're not talkin' to me. I might as well go on home then."

"Might as well," I said, briefly cutting my eyes over the top of the magazine. Pop got up and walked out of the terminal, never once looking back.

I read the magazine and two more while waiting for the bus back to Melbourne. The six-hour journey was shortened by the multitude of thoughts banging around my head. I just wanted to leave them all behind, just as I had left behind the box that my father told me contained the entire Murphy stake. I really didn't want any part of what was in the box.

Chapter 18

The Murphy stake arrived by certified mail three days later. I tossed it irreverently onto the sofa for three or four days before looking at it again. I was getting physically stronger every day, but mentally had a few lapses of strength. I thought about seeking professional help just to cope with what went on in Ocala, but I really didn't want to be analyzed. I just wanted a way to restore my pride. No shrink could give me that. A stranger couldn't make me feel better.

Boredom drew me out of the condo after six weeks of recovery. I felt a little relief to be home where I could drive anywhere with anybody at anytime and not worry about repercussions. I drove the short distance from my waterfront condo to the Galleria Mall. I hadn't been in a mall in ages, mostly because shopping malls were a social place, not a place for the serious shopper. I ventured out anyway, craving contact with people who were like me.

I started in the Tea and Read bookstore. It was small and intimate compared to Books-O-Rama. I walked through slowly, looking for anything that might interest me for a week. Mystery novels used to be my favorite as a kid. As a young adult, I didn't have much time for entertainment. I was focused on succeeding in medical school. I walked to the self-help section and began browsing books. The self-help section was adjacent to the two small shelves of tagged African-American interests. It was difficult to tell where self-help ended and African-American books began.

I ended up leaving with a copy of *Your Blues Ain't Like Mine* neatly tucked under my arm. I paid cash for the novel on my way out of the retailer. As an afterthought, I returned to the shelves to look through the different versions of companion Bibles, as a final search before leaving. When I walked out, there was no attendant at the counter. I passed through the sensors and heard a little chiming noise. I didn't pay much attention to it, and continued down the mall corridor, in search of another distraction. I was stopped by a young man, maybe 23, and asked to return to the bookstore. "For what?" I asked as I followed anyway.

When I arrived back at the book vendor, a mall rent-a-cop was standing in what seemed to be a combat readiness stance.

"Sir, do you have a receipt for that book?" he asked with drill sergeant panache. I searched the book and my wallet for the receipt. I couldn't find the receipt in either place.

"I paid cash," I said still calm, but concerned. My defensive fail-safe mechanism turned on. Before my trip to Ocala, I had no such thing.

"Cash purchases get receipts too," interrupted the clerk. His tone was accusatory.

"Perhaps someone made a mistake. My name is Dr. Kenneth L. Murphy, and I'm telling you that I paid with a twenty and two fives." The two men conferred with their eyes. I could tell that neither one believed me.

"I need you to come with me," said the mall security guard as he grabbed my arm. His eyes flashed blue steel.

"I'm not going anyplace! Take your damn hands off of me, cracker!" His reaction caused me to instinctively reach for his throat. His pupils dilated as oxygen deprivation began to set in. Adrenaline tightened my handle on his throat. I began to rant to him like a psychopath.

"Where's *your* receipt, punk? Don't you ever put your hands on me again! Oh, not so brave without your friends, huh faggot?!"

Background sounds intensified. "Let him go, sir. You're killing him. He's dying!" The command got louder and louder. Returning reason finally loosened my grip.

"Don't you ever put your 'f''ing hands on me!" The security guard crumbled to the floor holding his throat and gasping for air. A young lady surfaced from the shelving and asked what happened. She was the morning supervisor.

The twenty-three-year-old told her that he'd called mall security when he realized that I stole the book.

"I rang him up, idiot," she said.

"He didn't have a receipt," the clerk countered.

The supervisor went behind the counter and tore off the receipt and showed the clerk. He was adamant that he had no way of knowing that I paid for the book.

"The sensor sounded the alarm," he continued.

"I manually entered the sale. The barcode was all screwed up. Next time, call me before you go into superhero mode," she scolded. She turned to me, "Sir, I want to apologize." She opened the register to give me back my money. "The book is a gift for your troubles."

I was still clenching and tense, but I could speak. "You shouldn't have to pay for someone else's mistake."

I walked out of the store, in shock that a young man almost lost his life for having blue eyes and pale skin. I'd never behaved this way before, not even in my impetuous youth. I was angry at his skin. I immediately ended my mall experience and went directly home.

When I arrived home, I poured a midday drink—Martell cognac. I was swishing around my second drink when my adrenaline rush began to noticeably subside. I added a Valium for good measure and reclined in my Italian leather Lazy Boy, reflecting on my life before and after my visit to Ocala.

I would have never thought in a thousand years that I, Dr. Kenneth L. Murphy, could ever experience the life of average black folks. There was nothing average about my family; it stood to reason that there was nothing average about me. I came from good stock of exceptional people.

****

My father was bold. He said he was born that way and never felt restricted by unspoken or spoken race rules. Ms. Caldwell said that Pop got away with stuff that other blacks couldn't get away with because of his light skin, wavy hair, and straight nose. Pop called Caldwell's analysis bullshit.

"Most of the niggas in Ocala," he said, "are afraid of what white folks say they gonna do. I ain't scared of none of them. I'll do whatever I have to do to get what I want. That's what makes me different than these scary niggas around here."

Momma was altogether different. She was black but comely, as the Bible says. She came from a long line of educated Northerners many of whom were trailblazers in the arts and sciences. Momma was groomed to be the wife of somebody special. Pop said that he wasn't that special somebody, but her ride was late and he took advantage of the situation. They'd joke like that all the time.

Ocala was always too small for Momma. She was born in Harlem where black men and women read Thoreau and discussed Liberia. Momma saw the South as a place to prepare for intellectual leadership when the violent struggles up North subsided. That's how she ended up in Ocala. She never intended to stay and never intended to fall in love with Carnell J. Murphy, but like Daddy said of Ocala: "This place has a way of sucking you in."

We were privileged Negroes in Ocala. We played the piano and studied everything from engineering to philosophy under Momma's tutelage. She was biding her time until she could launch her bright boys directly into black nobility.

Pop kept us humble. Although he could afford most of the amenities Camden provided his family, Pop said that we didn't need them. He preferred to make quiet investments in us, instead. Each summer Momma, Mathew, and I would make a trip up North. Momma would point out Dr. So and So this and Professor So and So that. She'd always end by saying, "Children, I know his or her family, and they are no better than us." My father would join us when he could.

Mathew's death changed everything. Momma wanted to hide me up North and Pop didn't. They'd talk in code at the table about whether or not they were going to send me to boarding school. Pop argued that sending me to boarding school would only delay the inevitable encounter with racism or worse yet give me the false impression that education exempted me from the normal perils of colored people in white America. He thought that hiding me in school would do little to prepare me for what I'd face as a black man. They decided instead to keep me close to them and then, when the time came, send me to a historically black college. Conversations with Pop during my infrequent visits to Ocala made me remember some of that.

Growing up, I really didn't have any problems worth mentioning. We lived in a quiet area that was neither black nor white, just Murphy. Most of my life after Mathew's death was spent on our property. I was rarely allowed to go to Murphy's Grove like Mathew had, but we'd go to the lake fairly often. Black families knew and respected my father so much that I was never teased about my light father or my dark mother. Pop's discipline helped me when we had an occasional encounter with white folks. I learned to deal with them on a business level. Time and change wore away my business disposition, allowing me to accept and offer friendship to people of different backgrounds.

When I went to Florida A&M University, it was a continuation of my life back home. I was respected, admired, or feared for my light skin. I became a social chameleon. I fit in anywhere and everywhere, living in a beige world of neutrality. I found myself to be less threatening and more acceptable this way. If fair skin provided me with access, intelligence improved my situation.

A medical school diploma was an all access pass, and the University of Florida gave me ample opportunity to use it. Race, by and large, had been a non-issue for me. In fact, I found that I had more in common with white folks than black folks. The choices that my parents made, in truth, *had* exempted me from carrying the full weight of my brown skin. I never considered that the one place my magic mantle wouldn't work was in Ocala.

****

The recorder was flashing red, meaning that there was a message waiting. I pressed the button to hear the message. Nobody in Lauderdale knew that I had returned; I hadn't called anybody. The message played.

"Kenneth, I was calling to see if you got the package. And, Camden's daughter wants your telephone number. Call me back when you get this message." It was Pop. I didn't feel like calling back. He'd just have to wait until I took care of me. He called back several times before I returned his call later that night after finishing the entire liter of VSOP.

I dialed Pop's number. "Yeah, you called," I said to him when he answered. The liquor had removed some of my manners and most of my respect.

"Don't talk to me like we're goddamn friends. I'm your father."

"*Um-humm*. What do you want *father*?"

"Did you get the box?"

"Yeah, man, it's somewhere around here."

"What do you want to do about Camden's daughter? She wants your phone number."

"Give it to her. I don't care."

"Son, what's got in to you?"

"Three broken ribs, a fractured jaw, and a concussion, that's what got in to me."

"That ain't my fault. I told you not to mess with those crackers," he said. I hated when he did that.

"No, you're wrong. It *was* your fault and you know it. That's why you couldn't face me in the hospital," I said, while gulping the last of the cognac.

"I'm not afraid of any man. I just had somethin' to do—that's all."

"Sure. Whatever you had to do was more important than making sure that your son was all right? That's garbage, Pop!"

He hung on to the phone.

"Hey tough guy, I'm talking to you! Nothing to say, Pop, huh?"

After a long pause he said, "Son, it's okay to blame me if that makes you feel better."

"Since when do you care about the way I feel? You didn't think about me when you shot Kennelly."

"Why should I? That was 'tween me and him."

"You didn't think about me when you told the town that I pulled Miller out the river either—did you?"

Silence.

"How about when you let Miller die in the lake? Did you think about me then? DID YOU? I didn't think so. Carnell J. Murphy, a coward. You always said you can tell what a man is by his deeds. I know what you are."

"I didn't kill that boy. He drowned by himself in the lake."

"*Liar*. Miller drowned in the river."

"No, son, he drowned in the lake and I took him to the river to keep the peace."

"Were you there when he drowned?"

"Yes, right after he went under for the last time."

"You could have helped him," I mumbled, half high.

"I wanted to, but it was already too late. The water had already taken him down. He wasn't movin' when I fished him out. I tried to breathe life back in him, but he just laid there like a dead puppy. I wish your mother were alive. She'd tell you the same thing."

"You let him drown. On purpose you let him drown because he called you a nigga. 'Nigga help, help me nigga.' You were striking back at

Camden for not taking Mathew to the hospital, first. You wanted revenge—didn't you?"

"I'm no child killer!" Pop answered, his voice elevated by anger. I thought that he'd ask me how I knew that Miller used the word *nigga.* He ran by my statement like a mile marker on the Florida Turnpike.

"You're lying about something. Why would you move his body to the river?"

"You really don't know Ocala," Pop said. "If that boy were found at the lake, whether it was accidental or not, the white folk would have acted like the coloreds killed him. There would have been problems, big problems. At the river, everybody accepted Miller's death as an accidental drownin'. White kids ain't got no business at a colored lake without their parents. Your Momma . . ."

"Momma what?"

"Never mind. I just wanted you to remember your promise. Don't open the box until I die. Then, do nothin' for at least ninety days. Bye." Pop hung up before I could ask another question.

Chapter 19

The next day, old Dr. Shaw called from Charles Drew Hospital. Daddy had passed out in Murphy's grove some time during the morning. Dr. Shaw thought it was a good idea to come right away. I thanked him for calling, but would not commit to going back to Ocala.

"Carnell's raising hell. He doesn't want you to come back here, son, but I think it's best that you do. God may not spare him this time," explained the doctor.

"I'll see what I can do. In the meantime, please keep me posted on any changes in his condition," is all I could say. I was still stinging from the beating and the fact that my own father wouldn't come to the hospital to check on me.

The call to my father the night before was enough opportunity for closure for the both of us. I didn't need to rush to his bedside to ease my conscience or his. We'd said what needed to be said. I prayed for him not to suffer. I hoped for mercy and a swift, clean strike of Gideon's sword. I kept hoping while I packed, unpacked, then packed again.

I packed light because I didn't intend to stay long, three days tops. I had a black suit, boxers, and a ration of jeans. I pulled my car out of the garage and lowered the top. I stopped at the Amoco for gas and a pack of Doublemint, when I got the feeling that I'd left something back at the condo. I went back to make sure that the stove was off, the iron unplugged, and incense was out. I tripped over the damn box when I leaned over the machine to change the outgoing message. *What the hell*, I thought. My phone number was unlisted and only my friends had the number anyway.

"This is Kenneth. Please leave a message. I'll get back to you as soon as I can. If this is an emergency, I can be contacted at 407 366-4241 in Ocala." I picked up the box and headed for my car, box in hand.

I had vaguely remembered where Charles Drew Hospital was. I called Cousin Margaret so that she could direct me there from the turnpike. I couldn't remember ever going there as a kid. Dr. Shaw made house calls in those days. Momma and Daddy knew enough practical first aid to take care of most problems. The more complicated situations would warrant a call to Dr. Shaw, who would sometimes visit and other times call in a prescription that one of my parents would pick up at Reilly's Pharmacy. Not much had changed in forty years.

Dr. Shaw looked good to be ancient. He seemed a lot steadier than I remembered him being. He was confident, not frail at all. He was the dignified attending physician who still took an occasional patient to keep his skills sharp, or just as a favor to old friends.

The hospital looked great. It had been modernized to a fifty-bed facility. Most of the services performed were outpatient services or routine procedures. Charles Drew was not state-of-the-art, but it was well within the standards of good care.

Dr. Shaw met me at the information desk and personally escorted me to the room. He took the opportunity to talk to me about different things. He squeezed a lot into our short walk and elevator ride to room 218.

"I just want to put your mind at ease, son," said Dr. Shaw. "Medicine has changed so much over the year since I began my practice. You had to have a good set of eyes and lots of faith when I was in the trenches."

"I can imagine. Lots of my colleagues would be lost without ultrasound, CAT scans, and a full-service laboratory." I tried not to sound patronizing.

"I want you to know that your father has had all the modern tests. They confirmed what we already knew. He doesn't have much time. His liver is failing him. Right now, we're just trying to keep him comfortable."

"I appreciate what you've done for this community, but especially my family. I want you to know that you have my complete confidence, doctor."

Dr. Shaw smiled and winked. "You are a kind young doctor to try to spare my feelings. Your father told me that you had concerns about my diagnosis and treatment. I'm not offended at all. I know that you're a fine physician, but more importantly you're a good son."

"I'm glad you understand, Dr. Shaw," I said just as we were arriving at my father's room.

"Just take this advice from an old country doctor: the best tool that you have is faithful confidence. No amount of technology can teach you that. "*Shoooot*," he boasted, "I could have saved John Murphy from a premature death if they'd let me."

"How?" I asked.

"We'd been doing shunts around her for years when that boy fell on his head. All we had to do is relieve the pressure of the blood pooling in his skull by draining it. Simple procedure, really. Biggest problem then was infection. Damn shame to lose such a bright child."

I took my hand from the door handle and turned to Dr. Shaw. "Did his parents know that you could have relieved the pressure on his brain?"

"I'm sure your Momma told them or she wouldn't have asked me to go to Whitestone.

"What? Did you?" I asked, surprised at the revelation coming from Dr. Shaw.

"Son, I'm a healer. I don't care nothing about color, never have. Adelaide said she didn't want me touching her boy, so I just came on back. You know he stayed in that coma for a few days. We had enough time. It was the talk of the town."

"Maybe they just didn't have confidence in you," I said in disbelief that Camden and Adelaide Murphy wouldn't give their son a fighting chance.

"My work was good enough to save you." Dr. Shaw felt behind my ear. "See, the scar is still there. You had a nasty fall from the back of a truck. I think you might have been around two or three. We did the procedure on a table at the processing plant. As I recall, Adelaide and Camden watched. It was their truck that you fell off."

"Then they knew that you could do it," I said sadly.

"Yes, they knew," said Dr. Shaw. "God bless your momma; she was a good woman. She tried to get them to do the right thing for their son even though your daddy told her to respect the decision that Camden and his wife made. Yes sir, you are very lucky to have had such good parents."

I pushed into Daddy's room. He looked as though he was halfway to heaven. I reached down and hugged him, whispering, "I'm right here, Daddy, I'm right here."

"Son," Daddy whispered back, "what are you doin' here?" There was a hitch in his voice as he continued his message to me. "Well, since you're here, take me home."

I looked over at Dr. Shaw to get his approval for Daddy's request. He nodded his head slowly before turning to leave. Daddy's death wouldn't be a routine passing for anyone in Ocala. He had affected everyone, one way or another.

Chapter 20

Well-wishers lined the entrance to the hospital. Daddy was treated like a local celebrity. Work in the hospital seemed to pause momentarily to mark my father's departure. I thought of Bobby Kennedy's cross-country train ride to Arlington National Cemetery as the orderly wheeled Daddy to his departure. Nothing was missing except old Glory snapping in the wind.

I opened the passenger side door of my car and pushed the wheelchair the last few inches to the curb. I locked the wheel position to steady the chair for his transfer. I bent over to help him, but he waved me off as he called upon his reserve strength for a dignified descent into the convertible. He didn't have enough to complete the move by himself. He turned back toward the observers and waved one last time as if to say, "Don't worry; I can do this alone." He summoned what energy he had left and completed the act. It took a heavy toll on him to maintain his independent image.

I drove the distance from the hospital to the house without uttering a single word, neither did my father. He preferred to listen to the whistling wind and feel the sun's caress on his face. Neither he nor I wanted to ruin the moment with idle conversation about things that couldn't be changed no matter how we both wanted them to. I respected his position and never so admired his ability to boil an issue down to its bare, unadulterated essence. He was dying and practically dead. His priority was to take in a last breath of life, one that would carry him across the river for the last time.

I pulled up behind his truck on the side of the house and shut the car off. I exited slowly just in case Daddy wanted to ask for help, but I made no attempt to help without at least a gestured request. Instead, I walked the number of stairs leading to the porch and opened the front door. I gave him a few minutes before making an excuse to go back to see if he was all right. He sat in the exact same position he had when I had gotten out of the car. The only change is that the passenger side door was ajar. I reached under the steering wheel to open the trunk and remove my overnight bag, leaving behind the garment bag containing my suit, shirt, and an alternate pair of trousers. I gave him more time to ask for help, but he wouldn't. I closed the trunk and then went into the house where I stayed, as hard as it was, until he called.

"Kenneth,"

"Yes Daddy."

"Bring me a glass of lemonade."

I checked the refrigerator for the ever-full pitcher of lemonade. It was empty and there wasn't even one lemon in the house. Since I was a boy, I'd never known a time where there was no lemonade in the house. I made iced tea and added fresh squeezed orange juice and pulp. I took his favorite mayonnaise jar and filled it with cracked ice just the way he liked it. The ice split into smaller pieces when I poured the warm drink over it. I added more ice and more sugar and then walked it outside to Daddy who was still sitting in the car with his leg hanging out of the open door.

"Sir," I called with a soft voice. I didn't want to startle him. He opened his eyes slowly, blinking quickly to clear his blurry vision. I handed him the sweating glass full to the rim.

"Thank you, son." He pulled the mayonnaise jar to his lips and sipped. He sipped again just to confirm what his palate told him after the first swallow. "This is not lemonade."

"There wasn't any lemonade left and there were no lemons to make another pitcher. I improvised."

"I would have preferred sugar water or just plain iced tea. Take it away," he said ungratefully.

I took the full glass in the house and poured its contents into the sink without hesitation. I sat down at the piano staring at Momma's picture. She was smiling again, smiling her famous *never-mind-baby* smile. I understood and let Daddy have his time.

I washed my hands and began to cook dinner for the two of us. I made fish and grits. I found some okra and fried them so that they wouldn't be slimy. I set the table just as my father had done the first night of my last visit. Mathew and Momma had their setting as they had before. I called Daddy through the bedroom window. "Dinner's ready," I said. He grunted his acknowledgment. I waited for twenty minutes and then shouted again, "Daddy, I can't keep this food warm forever. The grits are stiffening up again." He was quiet this time.

I walked outside into dusk. Daddy had been sitting in my car for the entire three hours since our departure from the hospital. He must have tired of looking at part of the backyard and the dense trees growing toward the back porch. He was sleeping again. I didn't ask him anything this time. I leaned him forward and put one arm around his back and then tossed his arm over my shoulders. I picked him up like a ninety-pound infant and carried him into the house. He awakened just as we were passing through the living room toward his bedroom. "I'm hungry," Daddy said. I lowered his legs to the floor and helped him to his seat at the table. Funny, he didn't complain about being carried.

"Daddy, bless the table," I said as I waited quietly for him to find an appropriate prayer. He spoke through the twilight of pain.

"It's your turn, son. You're the man of the house now." He sat patiently waiting for me. I racked my brain for a good one as the seconds ticked away. I began cautiously.

"Lord only you have the power to change bitter fruit into sweet nectar. We know not why you have seen fit to work your wonders for this family, but we appreciate your tender mercies this day as every day. Hear this prayer, in the name of our redeemer and savior, your beloved son, Jesus Christ. Amen."

I looked at Daddy to see if he approved. He picked up his fork. Without eye contact, he whispered, "Your mother would be proud."

And so are you, I thought.

After dinner, Daddy wanted to sit on the back porch so I helped him to his seat. As he sat down he let out a sigh that sounded like it came more from his spirit than his diaphragm. His breath was like jasmine after a soft spring rain, sweetly angelic. Daddy's body hunkered down in the chair and he held on firmly to the armrests, preparing to launch himself like a butterfly from its hard cocoon. He was looking into distant light again.

Daddy pointed to a spot in the backyard. "Over there, son," he said. "Over there is where I want you to put this tired shell. I'll be close to your mother but far enough away for my wings to open up. I need space, lots of space 'cause I'm gonna have some big ol' wings."

"How big, Daddy?"

"Real big. I need big wings to catch up with your momma. I bet she has the biggest damn wings in heaven."

"Daddy, I don't think Ocala city government allows yard burials anymore."

"I'm not asking Ocala. I'm askin' my son; that's who I'm askin'." Daddy turned to me and locked his gaze before speaking again. "And, when a Murphy gives his word . . ."

"I know, I know. It's always good," I cut in.

"That's right, good as money in the bank. You better get some sleep. You're gonna have a big day tomorrow. You'll need your rest. Do me a favor before you go to sleep . . ."

"Yes, Daddy, what?"

"Call Camden and tell him that I'm askin' for him to come here tonight. I need to see him tonight, okay?"

"Okay, but are you sure he'll come?"

"He'll come. He has to come. He really doesn't have a choice. He'll understand."

"All right, I'll call right now."

"You do that."

I dialed Camden's number and Terri answered the phone.

"Terri, this is Kenneth. Please put your father on the phone.

"He's sleeping. What do you want him for?"

"I don't want him, my father wants him. Wake him up."

"I'm sorry Kenneth, I can't. He wasn't feeling well today. He just fell asleep after a good dose of tonic. I don't want to wake him up."

"It's very important. My father needs to speak with him."

"Where are you calling from?" Terri asked

"From *home*," I answered.

"Will I see you again?"

"I don't know. I only came back because my father's very ill. Dr. Shaw called me and told me that the old man doesn't have much time. I couldn't let him die by himself."

Terri slowed me down, "Other than that you wouldn't have come back, would you?"

"Terri, I—please put your father on the phone. This is a dying man's wish. Could you do that for me?"

"Do it yourself, Kenneth. I'll be here." Terri hung up the phone. I called back several times, but the phone just rang and rang.

"Is he comin'?" Daddy asked.

"He's on his way," I replied.

"Good."

"Daddy, I have to step out for a minute. Will you be all right until I get back?"

"Yup, I'm not goin' anywhere 'til I see Camden Murphy. I'm gonna have to wait on him. He's slow as hell since his wife died."

"Okay, I'll be right back."

I spun the tires quickly backing out of the gravel driveway, en route to Murphy's Grove. I knew that Daddy heard the rubber hit the pavement as the revved up engine pushed down the road. Why Terri wouldn't honor my father's deathbed wish made me sink the accelerator to the floor.

Camden was dressed by the time I arrived. He didn't look like he had much tonic. His eyes were clear and alert. He was sitting on the porch as if he were expecting me.

"Camden, did Terri tell you that my father wants to see you?"

"No, but I heard her on the phone. I wasn't sleeping soundly when you called. Where is he?"

"He's at the house. You can ride with me."

"That would be fine, son; that would be fine."

Camden came off the porch. He moved much more confidently than he had when he visited me in the hospital or when I saw him in the grove. He opened the door and plopped down onto the seat. He slammed the door with authority before saying, "Let's go."

Terri gazed over the porch railings as though her parents had left her home alone. I could tell she wanted to go and was equally sure that she'd follow. I waved at her as I turned to leave the property and Murphy's Grove.

Camden had a bottle of tonic pushing up out of his left pocket. I wouldn't have noticed it, accept that when I shifted into fifth gear, my watched banged the bottle. "What's that?" I asked.

"A bottle of Dr. John's Tonic. I've been saving it for a special occasion."

"This is a special occasion. This is your first time to my parents' house, isn't it?

"No, I've been to their house twice before," Camden said as if ducking down a dark alley in the seedy part of town.

"When was that Camden?"

"Once after my father died. The second time was when my first son died. If you want to know more you'll have to ask your father."

"Fair enough," I said, pretending to be satisfied with the partial answer that he'd given me. "Is that when my mother asked you to donate your son's liver to save my brother?"

"Hurry up, Kenneth. We don't have much time. Talk less, drive more."

"So you're not going to tell me if I'm right?"

Silence was an unequivocal response.

We arrived at Daddy's house minutes later. Camden opened the door and let himself out. He pulled himself up by holding on to the seat. He walked up the stairs as though he was going to walk through the house. He changed his mind and walked back down the stairs and around the house until he came to the back porch. I followed him.

Daddy pulled himself up in the chair. Camden's skin reflected some of the light from the lantern suspended from a hook twisted into the back wall of the house.

"Murphy is that you?" Daddy called

"It's me, Murphy." Camden responded.

"Where is my son?"

"Right here." I walked into the light, but my skin wasn't nearly as reflective as Camden's. "Daddy, I'm here," I said again.

"This is between Murphy and me. Go back in the house, son. Better yet, go for a drive or somethin'. We need some privacy.

"Yes sir," I said reluctantly. I walked past my father and into the house. Within ten minutes, I heard the arrival of another vehicle. It was Terri. I met her on the front porch. I sat in the same chair that Daddy sat in when he shot Kennelly.

"What are you doing here, girl?"

"Checking on my father. I wanted to make sure my father is safe," Terri replied.

"What's that supposed to mean?"

"Well, how do I know that you won't try to get revenge on my father for what happened to you at the river?"

"*Happened* means that it was an accident. Since when is revenge an accident? If *I* wanted revenge, I wouldn't sneak up on him or you. We're not cowards in this family," I said.

"Okay, Kenneth Luke. I can't argue the point. It was that for sure, but you have to believe that I wanted to stop it before it happened."

"Why didn't you?

"It was too late. Jim and some of the other Night Riders had already made up their minds that Kennelly's shooting had to be avenged."

"Jim? Jim the police officer?"

"Yes."

"Now, I've heard it all. How could a police officer do this? I thought Jim liked my father."

"He does . . .as much as he can like any black man . . .but folks in these parts are big on loyalty."

"Loyalty to whom, Terri?" I yelled.

"To white people, Kenneth, to white people. Kennelly wanted your father dead. Jim refused to kill your father—he said it wasn't right to kill an old man that was sick already. The compromise was to hurt you.

"Why me?" I asked.

"It was easier than harming your father—they liked one another. He felt that you'd be a better example than a dying old man. Besides, he was jealous that I'd allowed you to touch me.

"I never touched you."

"You touched me in the processing plant. You kissed and caressed these," Terri said as she cupped her breasts. "And, I told Jim about it."

"I don't remember seeing him in the crowd," I said.

"He was there. He was the one who called me whore. He dragged you to the clearing."

"Jim? Jim the cop? He'd let me die for you?" I said in disbelief.

"No, he stopped them from killing you after they beat you for awhile. He's the one who fired the shots that saved your life. Jim helped my father get you to the hospital." Terri's eyes filled with water and began to drip slowly down her cheeks. Her tears did nothing to calm my fury.

"He broke his oath to uphold the law over a chick? I don't believe it!

"How did your father know that this was going to happen to me? How, dammit!"

"Please don't hurt him. Please Kenneth don't hurt him. He's not well.

"HOW?"

Terri was sobbing incessantly. She crumbled on the porch stairs. I went to the edge and looked down at her. She was pathetic.

"My father saved your life. Kennelly's son was going to kill you."

"That kid—me—Kennelly's son? Oh my God. He works at the hospital."

"Yes, at the hospital. After that didn't work, he was supposed to put something into your I.V., but Daddy talked him out of it. Kenneth, my father stayed at your side in the hospital until you regained consciousness," Terri said.

"You still haven't answered the question. How did your father know?"

Terri didn't want to answer the question, but she knew that I wouldn't stop pressing her until she did. Her voice faded as she said, "He's a Night Rider."

I hustled down the stairs as fast as my injuries would let me go and slid around the side of the house to the backyard. It was pitch black in the area where the pail and gun rested, but I found it in the darkness. I lifted the rusted metal bucket and felt for the cold, black steel. I opened the gun to empty the chamber and dropped the clip to the ground. I walked into the backyard clearing so that I could see Camden's eyes when he pissed on himself. The porch was empty. Camden and Daddy were gone—more than likely into the woods.

I hobbled through the brush, calling out to the men, but they didn't answer me. I picked up speed as I jogged left and then right, but I could not find them. Perspiration beaded my forehead and soaked the back of my shirt. I stopped full at the lake and looked over the calm water. The lake was still, not a ripple in it. Where did they go?

I walked back to the house. Terri came through the house to the back porch, looking into the woods. "Where's my father," she asked, as if I had shot Camden like a wild moose.

"I don't know," I said, drunk on adrenaline and determination. "But, I WILL find him." I was subtly massaging the trigger of the old 45 while talking to Terri. She noticed as her shifting shadow lifted from me and the light fell onto the gun.

"What are you going to do with that?" she asked. Terri's fear turned to foolish bravado as she loosened my grip on the gun.

"I'm hunting white rabbit."

Chapter 21

At dawn, Terri and I searched and found the men at an abandoned moonshine distillery, just a few hundred feet from the water's edge. Neither man was moving.

Terri ran to her father who was unconscious but breathing on his own. Mangrove roots formed a cradle that kept him in an upright position on the swampy soil surrounding the lake. The empty bottle of Dr. John's Tonic was inches from his hand. Terri prodded and slapped to awaken her father, but he did not respond. My father was eight feet away and lifeless. I didn't have to check to know that he was gone.

I stood over Camden and watched Terri unsuccessfully try to revive her father. Terri turned to me for help. She didn't have to ask; it was in her eyes. I kneeled in the muck and lifted Camden's eyelids. His pupils did not respond to the change in light. His breathing was shallow and his heartbeat was weak. "Get the bottle and bring it," I commanded as I lifted Camden with a fireman carry and headed toward the house. I'd seen his symptoms during my E.R rotation in medical school. He had overdosed.

I dialed 911 and spoke to dispatch while Terri covered him with a blanket she stripped from my father's bed.

"What's your emergency?" asked the dispatcher.

"Probable overdose on some opiate derivative. More than likely morphine," I answered.

"Was he on medication?"

"Yes."

"Do you have the bottle with you?"

"I have an empty bottle of tonic that I believe is the source of the drug. I'll give it to the paramedics when they arrive."

"How do you know that he overdosed on morphine?"

"He has classic symptoms. I am a physician. My name is. Kenneth Luke Murphy."

"Is the victim unconscious?"

"Yes. He disappeared last night around eleven. His pulse is low and his respiration is shallow."

"I just need to confirm you address. Please don't leave the victim. Is there anyone with you?"

"Yes, his daughter."

"Have her wait outside for the paramedics. They will be there in about twelve minutes. Stay on the line with me until they arrive."

"Okay."

Upon arrival the paramedics started an intravenous line, intubated Camden, and then gave him an injection to help reverse the effects of the morphine. They whisked him out the door. Terri was in shock.

"Go with your father," I said. She followed the paramedics and jumped into the back of the transport heading for Charles Drew. My father was still at the lake, dead, cold, and alone. The excitement knocked me off my feet. My head started to spin as I sat on the settee. Momma was looking at me from the black and white photo sitting atop the piano. I couldn't face her just then. My heart was racing. I went through the bathroom cabinet and found an empty bottle of tonic. I turned it upside down until the last few drops collected in the cap. I swallowed quickly and then waited for it to kick in. I calmed down within fifteen minutes.

My thoughts were clear thanks to Daddy's favorite cure-all. I found my way back to the place where Daddy lay. I cradle carried him back to the house. I put him in his bed and then gave him a sponge bath before dressing him in his favorite suit. He said it was the suit that won over Momma. He hadn't worn it in for a long time because of the weight that he'd put on from years of eating Momma's Southern-style, Northern cooking. Daddy said that he'd be able to fit in the suit one more time before he was put into the ground. I didn't know that he meant it, literally.

I called Dr. Shaw and told him that Daddy had passed on. He told me he was on his way to examine the body. He'd promised Daddy that he would submit the death certificate to the county medical examiner's office. I think he just wanted to say his good-byes to my father with whom he'd had a long and warm relationship. I told him that he didn't need to rush. Daddy wasn't going anywhere. I recommended that he finish his work and then come after hours so that he could go home afterward to mourn privately. He agreed and showed up late in the evening with a friend, Mr. Seawright, the carpenter.

Mr. Seawright shook my hand and then asked to see my dad. I pointed to the bedroom that Daddy slept in every night since my mother died. He didn't stay long. Mr. Seawright said that he didn't want to waste Daddy's time with a long good-bye. He said my father was a man of few words and wouldn't appreciate a big scene. I understood.

Mr. Seawright asked me to move the automobiles so that he could drive to the backyard. I moved both the vehicles and he drove his old Volkswagen van into the back, near the tree. He jumped out and opened the back of the van. Handmade coffin, shovels, and an axe were inside. He unloaded the tools before gesturing for Dr. Shaw and me to help him remove the coffin from the van. It didn't take us long. Mr. Seawright backed the van out of the backyard with ease and was gone, leaving Dr. Shaw and me to quiet reflection.

"I'm tired son, real tired. I've seen the brightness of the sunrise in the eyes of a newborn and I've seen the sun set on those same lives. I've seen too much and I'm tired. I want to rest—rest like my first son is resting in that room up there. I want to go home."

"Dr. Shaw, he loved you. You were like a father to him."

"Yes, Kenneth, and he was a son to me. I'm the only father he's ever known and he was my only son. I never had a chance to have my own children. I was too busy taking care of folks around here to worry about that. Lord, I'm not questioning you," he said as he looked into the night sky, "but why didn't you call me before you called my son?" Dr. Shaw wept.

"Can I do anything for you, get you anything?" I asked.

"Yes. Bury your daddy by this tree. He wants you to do it by yourself. He said not to let anybody stop you because this is Murphy land, the land of his birth and death. Promise me, son."

"I promise," I said.

"And a Murphy's word is what?"

"Good as money in the bank," I answered. I have some things I need to send you when you get back to Lauderdale. Call me when you get home, son."

"Okay, Dr. Shaw, I will." Dr. Shaw left immediately. I saw a glistening teardrop on his face as he walked through the kitchen light.

I waited until late afternoon before I started to get ready for the night dig. I took the lanterns out of the bedrooms and lit them so that I could see what I was doing. I took Momma's picture from the piano to keep me company and dragged Daddy's favorite chair from the back porch to the spot that Daddy had picked. It was almost ten at night when I remembered how Daddy told me to rest because I would need it the next day.

At 2 a.m. I was still digging through dirt, sand, and stone in what my father called his final resting place. My shoulders ached, my hands blistered, and my back creaked. I sat on Daddy's chair and looked at Momma's photograph. She was smiling that encouraging smile. It was the one she'd give me each time difficulties made me want to give up. Her words came back to me like an angel's song.

She said, "You are brown and strong like mahogany and redwood. You weren't created to wither during the heat of trying days; but, instead, to be a cool canopy for those who grow in your shadow." I struck the rock with a pickaxe and it split.

Terri came back. Her father had succumbed during the night. Two Murphy children alone in the world sought each other's presence and comfort. She didn't have to say anything. It was just the look on her face as she stood in the porch light.

I was honoring my father's wishes and had little time for mourning. I struck and shoveled, shoveled and struck. Terri sat on the chair looking into the hole at my diligence, wondering how I could keep going. Other men would have quit, other men would have licked their own wounds, but I was a Murphy man. At 3 a.m. Terri picked up a shovel and joined me in the grave. She tossed out rocks like a construction worker. By 4 a.m. we were four and half feet deep and spent. I climbed out of the hole and then helped Terri out. She was covered in dirt, but never looked so good to me.

I rigged up a pulley to lower the casket into the hole. Terri climbed the tree and drilled into a huge branch that extended over the grave. She twisted in the pulleys then threaded the rope. Terri helped me carry Daddy out to the backyard gravesite. I put him in the coffin, and then I put Momma' photograph on his chest. I nailed the coffin shut. I pulled his truck into the backyard and tied the free ends of the rope to the hitch. Terri guided me as the truck raised the casket above the hole. I allowed the weight of the light casket to pull the truck until it was at the bottom of the trench.

We finished backfilling the grave at 6 a.m. At 6:30 we were covered from head to toe in dirt, grass, and leaves, but sleeping, fully clothed, in each other's arms atop the bed. We didn't stir until 7 p.m.

The dig was nightmarish. It made me doubt whether my father was dead and buried. It made me question how I found our fathers, or if I'd found them at all. Aside from the dirt on Terri and me, I had no proof that this was reality. "What happened last night?" I asked Terri.

"My father died at the hospital," she answered.

"Sorry."

Terri was stoic. "What time is it? He's probably already at the mortuary. He never came out of the coma."

"Then, what are you doing here? Shouldn't you be with him?" I asked

"Where should I be? The man is already dead. Who would understand what I'm going through better than you?"

"What about your Uncle Paul, or other family members?"

"I didn't think about them. I was drawn here to you."

"Terri, I didn't know your father that well, but, by and large, he seemed to be an honorable man. I know you will miss him."

"Yes—I will."

"What are you going to do now that he's gone?"

"I'm not in a rush to make a decision. Thank goodness I have the business to run. I need to keep busy. What are you going to do, Kenneth Luke? Going back to Fort Lauderdale, I bet."

"Yeah, the sooner the better. I'm going to sell the business. Maybe Cousin Margaret will keep things going until I decide what to do permanently."

"When are you leaving?"

"I have to go through my father's things; might as well do it before I leave."

"You could sell the business to me, Kenneth. I can handle it if I hire a foreman to help."

"I'll think about it. I have no idea what the business is worth. It would be great if I could get someone to buy the house, land, and the business as a package deal."

I took a towel and washcloth from the closet. My clothes and hers were a mess. There was dirt tracked through the whole house. "Do you want a towel?"

"No, I'm going to go home to clean myself up," Terri said. "But, thank you for asking."

"Are you going to be all right? Grief has a way of creeping up on you when you're alone. We both know what happens when we bottle our feelings. They never go away. Negative energy spreads like cancer."

"You're right," she said as she came to her feet. "I'm going home."

"I'll be here for a few days," I said. "Close the door behind you, please. I'm going to take a shower, have something to eat, and then figure out what to do next."

"Kenneth? May I come back . . . I don't think I'll need to . . . but, just in case . . . .

"It'll probably be better if you call a friend or a family member. This is still Ocala. Your boyfriend is still a cop. And I'm still getting the hell out of town."

"Jim is not my boyfriend. I don't give a damn what people in Ocala think. And—and I wish I could go with you."

"What's stopping you? The rode is open to anyone who wants to drive it. You can go to anywhere you like, but you can't go with me."

"My roots are here Kenneth . . ."

"So dig them up and take them with you."

"The grove, Kenneth Luke, I can't . . . "

"—Believe me. The grove will go on like everything else around here, whether you live in Ocala or Kansas. "

"I don't know if I can handle this alone. I don't want to start . . . this is so hard . . .my dad—he was the best. He taught me everything. He missed my mom and the boys so much. He never made me feel, you know, I mean, I know he loved me so much; not because I was the only one left . . .I'm sorry . . . I know you don't want to hear this . . . you got your own pain to deal with."

I hugged her like a friend. She tried to be strong, but she was breaking. There were visible cracks in her emotional dam and tears trickled through. I squeezed her to plug the dam. She squeezed back with a *please don't let me leave* embrace.

Tenderly, I brushed the hair from her eyes. She looked so vulnerable. I had time for closure. I had time to reconcile my feelings. I knew my father was dying; he reminded me every chance he got. Camden's death was thrust upon her. Terri only got a chance to say good-bye to his empty shell. "Do you want company," I whispered.

"Yes, Luke."

I took a change of clothes with me. Our drive to her house was quiet and deep like the bluest ocean, the longest river, and the deepest lake. We were already too far from friendly shores to swim back.

Chapter 22

Terri drove us to her home. She parked the van in the gravel driveway then quickly exited to close the three-foot gate. I pressed my face against the tinted windows, just in case Terri's "friends" came to pay their respects to Camden or to finish the job on me that was started at the river. It was déjà vu with one exception: this time there'd be no surprise.

Was this another betrayal? I honestly couldn't answer the question. Stronger women than Terri had folded under the scorching light of loyalty, based on nothing more than race. Camden her father, by most accounts a strong and gentle man, failed to stand when it counted most. How could I believe that the daughter he raised possessed the strength that he did not? "Fruit," Daddy said, "don't fall far from the tree." We were both proof positive that Daddy was right.

Terri opened the door and gestured for me to follow. The livable space was huge. Although it felt strange, I pressed onward, more for curiosity's sake than chivalry. I had been in many houses over the course of my life, from penthouses to boathouses. None piqued my curiosity more than this one. Sick voyeurism nearly broke my neck. I scanned both sides of the room as if watching a Williams-Davenport championship match.

"Drink?" Terri offered. I nodded. Terri pulled a delicate and expensive crystal snifter from the cedar racks above the hand-made bar. She unplugged the etched decanter and poured a generous drink. "Is cognac okay?" she asked, as she handed me the half-full glass.

"Smooth," I said as I wet my lips, tongue, and palate. The delayed bite told me that it was very good, very old cognac. I recognized it. "French import?"

"I don't know," she replied. "I just like the taste." Terri reached under the bar for the original bottle. The blue label indicated that it was aged at least seventy-five years. In the cigar bars peppering the high priced waterfront hangouts in Lauderdale, the drink she poured me was more than fifty dollars a shot.

Before the next sip, I raised my glass in tribute to her choice of beverages. What irony. As a child, even on sweltering days, we couldn't get a drink of water out of a paper cup at the back door. Now, I'm sipping 75-year-old cognac from the best crystal in the house, while lounging in dirty jeans. I turned to a picture of Ms. Adelaide and said aloud, "She would not be pleased."

"No, I'm sure she wouldn't," Terri answered, turning to the same photograph. "Sorry, Momma, times have changed."

After finishing her first drink, Terri got ready for her shower. "Kenneth Luke," she called, "let me show you where the shower is."

"Thank you, but I'd prefer a good, hot bath. Is that going to be a problem?"

"No—I'd like that too, but the tub is not large enough for both us." Terri baited her hook, but black fish wasn't biting.

I followed her to the tub, where she told me that I was free to use any of the gels, soaps, and spirits that I could find. I turned on the hot water and filled the tub, pouring wintergreen alcohol rub and Epsom salts into the water. Scented candles lined the wall like paraffin pipe organs. Wood matches were decoratively displayed in an oyster shell dish next to the candles. I lit them. The melting wax filled the chamber with the aromas of lilacs and cinnamon. I turned off the light and opened the bathroom door to let the steam escape from the tub into the rest of the house. My soiled clothes fell to the floor and I slipped into the homemade hot spring.

I assumed Terri's shower was over when I heard Michael Bolton's in some distant part of the house. *Georgia On My Mind* helped to float my concerns away. Lazy arms spilled out of the porcelain vessel, while water slowly leaked from it, draining away anxiety.

The cognac-enhanced bath relaxed me so thoroughly, my eyes sealed shut. When they re-opened, Terri was leaning on the doorjamb with a glass of burgundy. "Can I come in?" she asked.

I curled my fingers yes and she draped herself on the rim of the tub. The flickering flame illuminated the ringlet of hair falling from her loose pin-up. She bent forward and swirled the water with her index finger. Even in the candlelight, I saw a single, perfect breast unwrap from its silken covering.

Dim light couldn't hide her sadness. She was in the quicksand of grief and being sucked downward inch by painful inch, despite the effects of wine and song. The glistening in the corner of her eye wet the mask hiding her loss. "Get in," I said. "It will make you feel better."

Terri lifted the robe and stepped into the tub, careful not to step on any of my vital organs. She sighed as salts and spirits in the tepid water worked her aching muscles. Terri turned her back to me and disrobed. I opened my legs so that she could sit between them. She leaned forward and pulled her knees up to meet her forehead. Knots in the curve of her back and the sweep of her shoulders begged for attention.

I patted, rubbed, or kneaded each visible ball of tension. She moaned as they began to soften. My periscope, surprisingly, never broke the surface of the water, though massages—giving or receiving—never failed to arouse me.

I was still very attracted to her beautifully feminine body—God knows I wanted her—but I couldn't bring myself to profit from weakness. If we were going to be together, I needed to conquer her like other woman I'd been with. There was no excitement in alcohol-induced surrender. The challenge was still in the chase.

After the massage, she stepped from the tub and patted her skin dry. I did the same then wrapped the damp towel about my waist. I'd left my change of clothes in the van. It was an unintentional oversight brought on by the angst I had from sitting in a tinted vehicle, parked behind a locked gate in a backwater town with a prominent white woman.

"Aren't you going to get dressed?" I asked Terri as she headed for the comfort of the family room.

"I'm comfortable—are you?" she asked. Her words were filled with innuendo.

"I—uh—I left my clothes in the van."

"Do you need them now?"

"It's either get them or stay naked under this towel."

"Why under the towel?" she said. We're alone and I don't mind. May I offer you another drink?"

"That's very kind of you—and yes, that would be perfect."

"I can toss your clothes into the washer, if you'd like," said Terri.

"Okay," I said. "Saves me from having to streak to the van to get my things."

"*Mmmm,* streak. Nice," she purred.

"Look, Terri, you're a pretty woman and I'd like to indulge, but I don't think the timing is right for either one of us." I watched her eyes to see if she agreed before saying anything else.

"Are you saying that we're not going to have sex? Sex relaxes me," Terri said with the heartless honesty I appreciate. "It doesn't have to mean that we're getting married, Kenneth Luke."

"I know. But, I have to ask myself if we'd be in the situation if our fathers hadn't died."

"Yes, we would," she said. "Maybe not today, but we would. We don't need an excuse to do this."

"You don't have to convince me . . . I just don't want any regrets."

"You talk too much, Kenneth Luke," she said as she slammed her tongue into my mouth, counting each of my teeth as she twisted, flicked, and probed from front to back. The phone was ringing, but she wouldn't stop to answer. We fell tenderly to the sofa in front of the huge Cape Cod window overlooking the Jacuzzi on the sun deck. The phone rang several more times before we recovered for round two. "Let it ring," Terri said. "I don't want to talk to anyone right now."

We fell asleep briefly after sexing. Empty condom packages lay on the coffee table like spent bullet casings. We were naked, salty, and tired from our indulgent romp. The clock on the stand flashed ten o'clock. I stirred, gently waking Terri who had been recharging for more. She brushed me with her free hand and the magic returned to my wand.

"I want you," she said, impatiently trying to get it in.

"Wait. We need another condom."

She was charged. "It's okay. I can't get pregnant," she said. I'd heard that before. She needed to give me more proof than that for me to trust her.

"Terri, open your eyes. What do you mean you can't get pregnant?"

"Put it in, baby. I have an I.U.D. Hurry."

Like a teenager, I kept a spare rubber in my wallet, which was in my pants, my pants, in the bathroom. "Don't move," I said while I streaked to retrieve my protection.

I was struggling to pull the emergency rubber from the tight compartment in my wallet when I thought I heard the sound of a car coming to a stop outside. I wasn't sure because the blood feeding my brain had been diverted. The leather compartment finally released the condom and I skated quickly through three rooms to get back to Terri. It was difficult enough putting on a condom while standing completely still, but nearly impossible in a full sprint. Terri was still squirming on the sofa when I returned.

I stood in front of the sofa to make the final adjustments to the rubber before climbing onto Terri. It just didn't feel right at the end, so I squeezed the remaining air from the tip. The empty, uncovered window exposed me to the uniformed man climbing the four steps to the top of the sun deck. The ambient lighting backlit my body and cast enough light through the window to see that it was Jim; and he definitely could see me.

"Terri," I said softly."

"Yes, baby" she whispered.

"You have company."

"Yes, make love to me."

"I said that you have company."

"What?" she said, shattering the mood. "Where?"

"Right here," I said, pointing out the window. Terri sat up. Her blood flush breast stared at Jim through the window. In a flash, Jim's face ran the gamut of emotions from shock to anger. His exaggerated, silent-movie expressions required no captions.

Terri unabashedly reached for the towel on the floor. She couldn't take her eyes off Jim, so I handed it to her while I remained brazenly visible, my flaccid flag waving in the air. She opened the door and walked out to have a few words with him while I headed for the kitchen cutlery. Shortly afterward, I heard the spinning tires of Jim's police cruiser madly propelling him into the night.

Chapter 23

Daddy's house seemed a better place to be. Try as I did I couldn't shake the feeling that Jim was coming back and that he might not be alone. I didn't want to hang around Terri's house waiting for him.

"What did Jim say to you?" I asked.

"Nothing?"

"Do uninvited guess usually knock on your back door?"

Terri searched for a believable answer. "It's not like that. Jim was concerned. He said he tried to call several times. You heard the phone ringing."

"Yeah, I heard it," I said from an emotional distance.

"He came to check on me. He had no idea what kind of shape I'd be in."

I faked a calm demeanor. "I understand. Let me get my things so that you can take me back to my house."

"I'm not ready for you to leave, Kenneth."

"Yeah, but I'm ready to go."

"That's fine, but I'm going with you."

"I don't think that's a good idea, Terri. Jim was pissed about us."

"That's probably more of a reason for you to stay here tonight. Just so that you know, he's wanted me to be his girl since we were children. How would you feel if you saw the woman you love naked with another man?"

"That can't happen, Terri."

"Why is that Kenneth?"

"I don't believe in love. Love messes up good relationships," I said.

"That's not true; you were married."

"That doesn't mean I was in love. I just needed a wife for sex and social occasions. Marrying her just made coordination easier."

"That's bull, Kenneth, and you know it."

"Okay, but I still want to get the hell out of here.

"You win. Let me take a quick shower then we can go."

"Take it when you come back. I'm only eight minutes away. You don't even have to come to a full stop," I said trying to rush her.

Terri cleaned the coffee table and fluffed the sofa cushions. "You're not scared—are you?"

"Scared is one thing, stupid is another."

"Relax," Terri said, "I'll be out in a minute. Have another drink if you want. The keys to the van are on the counter, just in case you want to put on your clothes before I'm finished." She disappeared down a small corridor and turned into one of the bedrooms.

I went to the other bathroom to get the shirt, pants, and boxers I left on the floor. Earlier, I took off my bracelet and pinky ring before getting into the tub. The top of the water tank was empty, so I checked the pockets of my pants. I shook the pants and the ring fell to the floor and rolled out of view into the corridor dividing the cluster of rooms. I flipped on the light; nothing but dust was on the hallway floor.

I opened the door to the room across the hall from the bathroom. It was a small sewing room. The walls were papered with floral pattern that made the room friendly and comfortable. Sketches and patterns of dresses and gowns were framed and hung as decorations on all unoccupied wall space. The shelf over the professional sewing machine was fitted with adjustable track lighting. On the top shelf were boxes, beautiful boxes.

I pulled one off the shelf and looked inside. It was a hatbox. I checked another; it had jewelry in it. I didn't hear Terri coming up behind me.

"Having fun?" she said sarcastically.

"Should I be," I replied, a little embarrassed for rummaging through Adelaide's personal possessions.

"This was my Momma's favorite room. I come in here when I want to feel her presence. It's just the way she left it. Daddy and I like it the way it is."

Jewelry sliding around in the box caught Terri's attention. She came closer and noticed the gleam. "Where'd you get those," she asked.

"They were in the box." The look on her face told me that I'd discovered treasures that she didn't know about. Terry raked through the rings, necklaces, broaches and bracelets. There was a small fortune in the box.

"These are beautiful, Kenneth. Momma must have stored them here for safekeeping."

"I'm sure," I said. "Makes you wonder what else is in this house." I thought about my parents' house, but especially the bound box that Daddy told me to open only after he was dead.

Terri pulled the other containers from the shelves and opened them as respectfully as I had. The next box had bond certificates and a few hundred dollars in cash. Other boxes on the shelf were empty or had sewing accessories in them. There were more boxes still; some stacked neatly on the floor others sitting in the small closet covered by a bi-fold door. I could tell by Terri's determination that we were not leaving until she'd opened them all.

She was possessed, tearing at boxes and the contents within. Most were filled with ornaments or design patterns. Terri found insurance policies, bank statements, and tax returns from years past. Most were her parents, but a small parcel of documents belonged to her grandparents who had built the house and business before Camden's birth.

"Let me see some of those," I asked. Terri was pouring over one particular document, which was pretty old by the looks of the deteriorating paper. As she read on, her body seemed to tighten up.

"Read those over there," she said as she turned her back to me, guarding the document from my inquisitive eyes. Her behavior caused natural curiosity to surge in me.

"It must be interesting reading. What is it?"

"Nothing to concern yourself about. It's family business." Terri carefully tucked the discovery into her purse. "I'll take you home now."

My red flag unfurled. Less than thirty minutes before, she wanted me to stay with her. Suddenly, she was a lot less hospitable. I decided to try again to loosen her up on the way to my parents' home.

As we drove to the property, Terri looked at me differently than she had before. Contempt returned to her eyes as if I were somehow responsible for her change in attitude. Perhaps it was my fault for opening Pandora's Box, but I hadn't a clue as to how anything that I'd done could be linked to a cryptic stash of aged paper.

"You don't have to tell me all the details, but what has you seeing ghosts?"

"I can't talk about it right now. I need to think."

"Is there anything I can do to help?" This simple question brought Terri back from her subconscious drift. For the first time since leaving her house she was looking at me, not through or around me.

"Yes," she said slowly.

"What is it?" I asked impatiently.

"Sell me your father's house and business." Her voice was Vincent Price-like.

"Where did that come from?"

"Well, Luke, you aren't going to stay in Ocala. This is not your home. You said so yourself. Selling me the house cuts your ties with this place. I know that's what you want—isn't it?"

I had seen Daddy negotiate enough deals to know that she was holding back information, critical information. I wasn't going to show my hand.

"I'm in no rush. This place pays for itself. There's no mortgage on the property, as far as I can tell. I was thinking that I'd hire somebody to keep the business going and keep the house in the family."

"Why do you want to do that? It's just a headache you're going to have to deal with eventually."

"You're right, Terri, but it's my headache."

We pulled to a stop in the front yard and talked a few moments more. Terri said that she was going home to rest and think. She'd only get about four hours of sleep before the sun came up. I didn't believe it would matter. I knew the look. She wasn't going to sleep any time soon. I got out of the van and walked the stairs to the front door. Terri drove off.

I put the key into the lock and turned. Just as the door swung inward, I heard the smack of the spring-action screen door slamming shut as someone passed through it. The sounds of fleet feet across the porch and down the stairs released a large dose of adrenaline into my blood stream. I ran toward the back door to get a glimpse of the intruder, but he'd already disappeared into the woods.

The house smelled like a gas station and there was the faint scent of smoke coming from the hallway leading to the bedrooms. I walked cautiously down the corridor and opened the door to Daddy's room. It was ablaze. Smoke poured out as the mattress and curtains were consumed. The fire was already too advanced for me to do anything but get out. I backed my car to a safe distance and watched my father's life work burn to the ground, taking with it all reminders of my mother and brother.

The smoke from the smoldering embers attracted a small crowd in the morning. Terri was among the curious onlookers. "Still want it?" I asked? I waited for her immediate response. The charred sub-floor caved in as the roof crash down.

"There's nothing left," she answered. "God, Luke, everything is gone. Did you have time to get anything out?"

"No. Pictures, papers, and piano—they're all gone." She looked relieved as she softly placed her hand on my shoulder as a comfort.

"You can stay with me for a few days," she whispered discretely, "while you pick through the pieces."

"Thank you, but I think I'm going home."

"Come by the house, Kenneth. I want to talk to you before you leave."

"Thanks. I'll be by. Maybe I *will* stay with you overnight," I said loudly to kick dirt in Ocala's face. It was my final act of defiance of the trailer-park ignorance that had destroyed more than an old, wood-framed house on concrete footings. Sadly, I wasn't feeling as sophisticatedly liberal as I had before I came back to be with my father.

Chapter 24

I howled like a lone wolf on an Arizona mesa. The full day of sifting through the rubble of memories left enough coal in my belly and fire in my heart to start one more blaze. Terri's gracious offer didn't appeal to me as much as it had earlier that day. There was no one around to punish by being with her. I just wanted to go home and put the bad memories behind me.

As I drove away from the place where my family home used to be, I thought about heading for the open rode, but a Murphy's word is his bond. The least I could do was to tell Terri that I'd decided to leave, make my apologies, and go.

Terri was sitting on the porch staring into the darkness when I arrived. I parked my car outside of her gate and walked inside to the concrete landing. I put one foot on the first rung of the stairs and leaned over, exaggerating my fatigue.

"How are you doing?" I asked.

"I don't know," she replied. "I guess all right."

"Hey, I'm the one who should be dragging."

"You're right. Guess I'm tired, too."

Terri stood to switch on the outside lantern before resuming the conversation.

"You're healing pretty well. The swelling in your jaw is just about gone."

It was the first time that she made reference to my injuries since the assault. "Yes, the body is an amazing machine," I said.

"You don't look like a man who's staying the night."

"That's true, but how can you tell?"

"You're pretty obvious. Your car is outside the gate and you're standing at the bottom of the porch. I guess I don't blame you."

"I don't know if I'm going to make it home tonight, but I'm definitely going to put some distance between me and Ocala."

"Some of Jim's friends are coming for me tonight," Terri said. She didn't seem concerned at all.

"What?"

"I guess burning down Carnell's house wasn't enough for them."

"Why don't you call the police for protection," I asked. After thinking about Jim, I said, "Okay, so I'm not the sharpest pencil in the box. What will you do?"

"This afternoon I put a no trespassing sign on the gate. I also got some bullets for this thing." She held up an old 45-caliber. "Recognize this?"

"Looks like my father's gun. I forgot all about it."

"I didn't." She paused before continuing. "If I see them coming, I swear I'll take them down."

"Suppose it's Jim?"

"If Jim doesn't want to die, he'd better phone first."

"I don't get it, Terri."

"What is there to get? I wasn't supposed to sleep with you—remember? People have a hard time forgiving that kind of thing around here, especially when it's a white woman and a black man. If you're leaving you better go soon. I don't want anything else to happen to you."

"That's very kind of you, but I can take care of myself. Are you sure you're going to be all right?"

"Uh-huh. They don't want to kill me; they want to make an example out of me. I've heard stories that they raped a white girl in Apopka for going with a black guy."

"I've heard enough, Terri. I suggest that you get out of town for a few days to let things cool down."

"Are you making me an offer, Kenneth Luke?"

"I wasn't, but if you want to ride with me, you're welcome. I'm going to drive south for at least an hour before I stop—maybe more."

"Let me get some things."

I sat in the car and waited for her. She was out in less than five minutes and, shortly thereafter, Ocala was in the rearview. We drove south for two hours before finding a Motel 8.

Our identities were somewhat obscured by darkness, but I took the added precaution of raising the convertible top before pulling into the parking lot. I wasn't sure if we were far enough from Ocala's grip to take chances. "Separate rooms," I said to the attendant without Terri's permission or consent. Terri offered no protest to my decision, but it wasn't long until she knocked on my room door. Despite my concerns, I let her in. She wanted comfort. She wanted me.

Terri mounted me, trembling with intensity as she threw her knee over my still body and lowered herself onto my saddle. She slowly loaded me into her depths. Breathy *ahhs* bubbled to the surface, melting away control and composure. As she took in more, bubbles turned to waves, waves to twitches and gasps. She fought for control of her body, but quickly gave in to uncontrollable shivers and shakes.

On her back, she surrendered to passion and settled into the bed. There, she let go of caution, and restraint washed away like desert dust in the undulating Nile. She was in a dream state, southeast of rapture.

Terri took all I had and never complained. She transformed my tension to passion; found small muscles that I'd forgotten about and worked them into butter. With flesh not words, we negotiated and compromised until the barrier between us disintegrated.

"It's okay," she whispered.

Without protection, it felt so natural. Walls began to fall one after another. I wanted to tell somebody how good it was; somebody had to know. I howled from the deepest part of my soul.

Terri slowed down as the pressure built in her bladder. After she burst, she slid out of our love-warmed sheets and scurried to the bathroom. I heard the toilet flush through the partially open door, then the rush of water spraying from the showerhead. Before disappearing behind the door, she whispered, "Rest. I'm not finished with you yet."

She was going to shower, going to wash off all that we had been to each other. I hated that it took only soap and water for her to make us go away, while I—I reveled in the wet spot like a kitten in a laundry basket. Each wrinkle in the sheet was a sensual distraction, refreshing and renewing my attraction to her. The sound of the locking deadbolt piercing the door frame called me to new opportunity.

Terri's purse lay on the desk. Folded papers sticking out of it were more than likely the documents that she'd withheld from me. I couldn't help it; I had to know what was written there. I read copies of two quitclaim deeds assigning fifty percent ownership of Murphy's Grove, the lake, and two houses to my father. A notarized letter signed by Camden Murphy's father, Maxwell, authenticated the deeds and provided further instruction. When the shower stopped, I quickly returned the documents to Terri's purse and reclined like a hero in a Harlequin.

But the energy had changed in me. It had become primitive and animalistic. I heard drums instead of violins. My kisses were fiery and hard. I wanted to get inside of her, probe her; that was my objective.

I hovered over Terri. Our bodies touched only at the hips. I was barely inside when I began small rhythmic strokes. I watched intently as she shut her eyes and tightened her hold on me, drawing ecstasy nearer. My strokes got deeper—more intense. Terri's hips dipped to accept me as her creamy legs rose into the air. I exhaled deeply, maniacally, with each thrust.

Terri's breasts were cold. She tried to pull my warm body to her, but my arms would not bend. Wiping the sweat from my brow, her hands slid from my face to my dew-sheeted chest. Wet fingers slipped around back, down my spine, and onto my sculpted seat. Her pelvic waves rolled in, sweeping me up like a riptide. "Too deep," she whispered.

Terri's words were Viagra to me, turning wood to iron. My rod vibrated like a tuning fork as blood continued to rush toward the tip. My breathing was shallow and determined, coming in short, deep grunts.

Terri's feet descended from the air to the ruffled sheets. She pulled her hands from the curve of my back and placed them at her sides, spreading her fingers into two stop signs that she used to signal that she'd had enough.

"Slow down, sweetheart," she said, inoffensively, but I kept pumping and drilling, drilling and pumping. Terri clenched the sheet as I bore down on her, hammering at her tender flesh. She couldn't take the pounding anymore. She put her hands against my chest and pushed forcefully. "Stop, dammit! You're hurting me."

I lifted Terri's legs onto my shoulders and folded her body in half, grinding diligently toward punishing self-gratification. I shifted my weight from my knees to my feet and hands in mock push-ups then I sunk my entire length into her, vanishing into her fragile feminine fabric. Terri's scream was long and shrill. My spear had ripped through Terri's spirit, and it bled tears.

I rolled off Terri without as much as a remorseful glance. My shower was business-like. Terri was in a fetal position when the bathroom door opened and I walked out. She tightly held the sheet wrapped about her body. Exhaustion and hurt sprinkled her face.

My assemblage of undergarments lay on the desk. I put on my T-shirt then drawers before sitting in the chair facing the bed. As I leaned over to put on my socks, Terri asked, "What's wrong?"

I stood to put on my pants and shirt. I buttoned down the collars and then ritualistically tucked my shirt into my trousers. I fastened my pants and then centered my belt buckle between the two front loops before responding to Terri. "You're white," I said coldly, as though it was a new discovery.

She sat up in the bed, drawing the sheet toward her chin. Terri knew that our love boat had broken free of its mooring and sailed on the seaward tide without us.

"Come here," Terri whispered while stretching her hands to me. She flattened her palm against mine and then slowly spread her fingers. She gently tried to pull me to her, but my spine wouldn't sway. Our fingers folded down on the back of each other's hand like a strange flower. She bent over and kissed my hand softly, sadly, as though this was our last time together. For a brief moment, the fire in her eyes dimmed to a filtered glow. She released me and stood fully erect, chest out, chin up, like a femme fatale in an old black and white. She flashed a look at her purse, and it was done. She knew.

"We can't do this anymore," she said.

I nodded, knowingly. I watched as she retreated behind cavalier armor. I was unwilling to pay the price to pull her back out. Only a lie of omission could keep the façade alive

"The deeds Terri, were you ever going to tell me about them?" My voice was laced with disappointment.

"Do you know what I've risked to be with you?" she asked, tilting her head with the weight of the question.

I didn't want to speak for myself, so I spoke for my family. "How long did you know about this?"

"Don't you care about us?" is how she didn't answer my question.

"'Love don't love nobody.'"

"What is that suppose to mean?" she asked, puzzled by the reference.

"Never mind—you wouldn't understand. My question to you is, how long have you known that my father owns part of the grove?"

"I'd heard rumors, but until I found these, I thought it was just one of Kennelly's scare tactics," she said, holding the papers in the air. "I had to find out if the documents were real." Her words fell on deaf ear.

"Let's get to business, Terri."

"Okay."

"The lake and what's left of my father's house and land belong to me. You can have the plantation. I want half of the profits from the grove in exchange for one thing . . ."

"What's that?"

"Add one line to that big Murphy's Grove sign."

"I can't do that. The place has always been Murphy's Grove."

"Then we'll sell the damn business. I don't really care."

"Okay, Okay," Terri reluctantly agreed.

"Tomorrow, the sign will read *Murphy's Grove, Camden and Carnell Murphy proprietors.*

I thought about asking Terri if any of the rumors she'd heard explained why Max gave property to my father, but I wasn't sure that I could handle what she'd say. I doubted if she'd tell me even if she knew. Maybe Daddy knew the answers to these questions. The Murphy stake, I remembered, was still in the trunk of my car.

"I'll be back in a few weeks with some documents for you to sign, just so there's no confusion about our agreement."

"That's fine," she said.

We were finished with our business, all of it. There was really nothing more to talk about except how Terri was going to return to Ocala.

"Are you coming?" I asked.

"Where?"

"Fort Lauderdale."

"No, I don't think so. I'm just going to go on back home in the morning. The funeral is Saturday and I have to be there. I think my father would have liked you to be there, too."

"I don't think so. It doesn't seem right after the things we did in his house."

"My house," she said. "Do you think Carnell would mind if he knew that I helped put him in the ground?"

After a long thoughtful pause I answered her the only way that I thought appropriate. "It's a good thing that both our fathers are dead. The two of us together would have killed them." I was standing at the door.

"I know."

"I gotta go, Terri." She waved as I twisted the door handle and walked out.

Neither one of us knew what to say. Somewhere else, under different circumstances, she and I could have had a relationship, maybe even a special one built on trust and honesty. I stood by the door and looked at her with the understanding that we could never be more than we were–cowards stealing a few pathetic moments in the dark. Our fantasy was cancelled—Ocala saw to it—and, it died as strangely as it lived.

I drove until the sun came up and then pulled over on the side of the highway, halfway to the Florida Keys. I popped the trunk to get my legacy from inside of the bound box. At the very bottom of the box was a time-tarnished envelope addressed: *To My Son.* It wasn't my father's handwriting; the strokes were two flowery for a no-nonsense man like Daddy. I opened the envelope and read the letter.

August 22, 1935

Carnell,

If you are reading this letter, I am already dead. You have a right to know who you are no matter how little this will matter to you as you grow up colored.

Although I could never acknowledge you in life, you are my first-born son.

Your mother worked for me. She served me faithfully and provided me comfort during some difficult days. She was a fine woman, smarter than most people I know. She helped me build this grove into a successful business. She would have been my wife if God hadn't cursed her with black skin, but of course he did.

I have provided for you as your mother requested, and a Murphy's word is like money in the bank. The house you live in will be yours as will part of the grove. You must never tell anyone, but work with your brother, Camden. Give him the respect you'd give any other white man.

Maxwell Murphy

The letter explained everything.

I put the car in gear and accelerated for the fast lane. I thought about the last few months, but mostly about Terri as I drove further south. I couldn't tell anyone about this, especially not Terri. It was better to just let sleeping dogs lie.